PRAISE FOR

LAZARUS

"Veronica Mars meets Encyclopedia Brown for the digital age. Two teenage sleuths solves crimes in this clever caper sure to engross even cozy mystery fans." —Lynn B, Media

LAZARUS

MARYANNE MELLOAN WOODS

Owl Hollow Press

Owl Hollow Press, Springville, UT 84663

Lazarus

Library of Congress Cataloging-in-Publication Data
Lazarus / M.M. Woods. — First edition.

Summary:
Margo and the late Hank team up to solve a local murder—Margo doing the detective work and Hank spying on suspects unseen—in tiny, god-forsaken Lazarus, Nebraska.

ISBN 978-1-945654-62-6 (paperback)
ISBN 978-1-945654-63-3 (e-book)
LCCN 2020943966

Cover design by Owl Hollow Press
Stock image SuperHerftigGeneral / Pixabay.com

OWL HOLLOW PRESS

for Johnny and Sara,
for everything, always

and for my mother
Joan Minner Melloan
who loved a good mystery

☼   ☼   ☼

ONE

MARGO

link plink. Plink plinka plink.
I'm trying to concentrate and my boyfriend Hank is lying on my bed playing the ukulele. Glasses low on his nose, noodling around, amusing himself. It's sorta sweet but mostly annoying.

I know I'm obsessing, but I want to look good for the first day of school. Put together. *Strong.* The opposite of the way I actually feel.

Plink plink. Stru-u-u-m.

Concentrate. The orange felt flower pin on the gray crop jacket over my dress (with chunky boots, that's a given) or just the magenta shrug? Or is it all too cutesy-thrift-store-punkette? Should I just wear black?

No.

I did that the year my mother died because I thought, *That's what you do.* And now here we are again. But I'm not that little girl anymore; I'm sixteen. And I refuse to dress like Margo Pierce, tragedy magnet. Because that's what everyone expects. Heads bowed, can't make eye contact, *Oh, the poor thing…*

How about orange pin *and* magenta shrug? Why not? How's *that* for Grief Girl?

"Ooh, very *bold*, very *now*," Hank simpers from the bed.

Fashion teasing from a guy wearing '70s wire rims and a ripped green Foo Fighters tee.

I cast him a look. "You know, you shouldn't even be up here."

"I shouldn't be a lot of places," he counters. "And yet up I turn like a flat gopher in the road. And you know you're always glad to see me." Hank smiles his crinkly Hank smile and I can't disagree with him. I am pretty much always glad to see him. He balances out my too-serious side. And right at the moment he looks so cute, I wish I could climb onto the bed with him and mess up my outfit. But of course I can't.

A smell wafts in from downstairs: bacon frying. *Are you kidding me?!* I head for the door.

I take the stairs two at a time, stopping for a second by the open window on the landing. A gust of wind snakes down Mac-Culloch Street, and there's something about that first cool breeze of late summer. Ruffling the lilac border in our side yard, making the rainbow spinner on Mrs. Peek's mailbox twirl madly. Blowing across the porches of all the weatherworn, comfortable old houses on our street. Advertising the deep freeze to come.

I hop down the last steps and swing into the kitchen where my dad's at the stove, already in his uniform. A strapping, gray-templed police officer focused lovingly on bacon—it's almost comical. Except it's not.

"You're throwing that out, Dad," I say.

"It's for you!" he insists. "You need a good breakfast on the first day of school."

His blue eyes are so determinedly cheerful, so rumply *Dad-ish*, I could almost believe him.

I love this man. It's been me and him, Team Pierce, slaloming life's curves together for seven years now. Picking each other up when we fall. Co-dependent in the best possible way. Which is why I say, dripping skepticism, "Uh-huh. Except I don't eat bacon and you know that. So then you say, *Well, it's already cooked. I might as well eat it.* Right?"

At this, he actually looks like he might cry, which is saying something for a police chief who can lift a pickup truck off a stray calf. I feel bad, but Dr. James has him on a strict low cholesterol diet and I am the Enforcer. If I don't do it, who will? I will not have him joining my mother anytime soon.

He turns off the stove and dumps the bacon and grease into the trashcan, grumbling the whole time. I get us both some whole grain cereal, which he looks at like it's the Black Death. I try to distract him.

"So, I bet you're glad summer's over," I offer, sitting down. Dad's always called summer "stupid season" in Lazarus. Firework injuries, diving board mishaps, 101 things that can go wrong at a barbecue.

"Oh, I don't know." He sighs. "Summer's the exciting time in my line of work. Chasing horny teenagers out of the cornfields. Real Clint Eastwood stuff." He pours his coffee.

"Well, there was one big event in Lazarus this summer," says Hank from the doorway. He's leaning casually on the door jam, like he's not being an idiot.

Goddamnit. I shoot him a look but he keeps going.

"Come on, it even made the *Norfolk Daily News.* Right between the Beef Council report and 'Teens Deface Dairy Queen.' I wish my mom had given 'em a cooler picture, and really, 'honor student' was a bit of a stretch…"

"Okay, Hank, that's *enough*," I hiss.

Dad looks at me. *Uh-oh.*

"Hank? Did you say *Hank*?"

Oh no. Here comes the worried look again. It's like the stress lines in his forehead just deepened. I blew it.

"Margo, why are you talking to Hank?"

Across the room, Hank shrugs—*oops.*

Dad's look shifts from worry to gentle sadness. "Honey, you have those counseling meetings set up, right? Did that first one help at all?"

I touch his arm, offer my most reassuring smile. "Dad, I'm *fine.*"

He's not buying it. He leans in, fixes me with the laser blue Chief Roy Pierce stare.

"You're talking to Hank at the breakfast table, Marg. And he's been dead for two months."

He has.

Hank hangs his head, a wave of toffee-brown hair falling over his glasses. He forgot he was dead again—he does that sometimes—and just jumped into the conversation.

I could tell my Dad, *No, really, he's actually here. As here as you and me.* Because I believe he really is. I'm just the only one who can see him.

But that's not going to fly. So I just smile my weak Grief Girl smile and look down at my orange and magenta ensemble, which isn't hiding anything.

TWO

HANK

O kay, so yes, I'm dead. But I'd like to think I still have much of my corporal charm. I'm stuck in this bloodstained Foo Fighters t-shirt, which is not an ideal look; who knew that you have to spend eternity in the last outfit you wore? But I'm still me, and I can still make Margo laugh, so... there's that.

Actually, I'm not feeling that charming lately. Because I am totally, absolutely, *extremely* dead, and I'm not happy about it. Everyone I love is like, *emotional toast*, and I'll never even f-ing graduate from high school. I'll forever be poor, lost Hank James, accidentally creamed by a Ford Explorer one summer night. And I'm so much *cooler* than that.

I won't get to cut the last day of school and skinny dip in the quarry, a time-honored tradition. The water June-cold, all your friends flapping around you—pure joy.

I won't go to the prom with Margo, which I know sounds lame, but it's not lame if you have it ripped away.

Northwestern is off the table, and my English teacher, Mr. Hawkins—who we'll get to later—said he definitely thought I could get a scholarship. And New York/Europe/groundbreaking journalism career/marrying Margo and the ensuing awesome Margo-Hank kids, cool house, etc.—all gone.

You suck moose turds, Carolyn Claypool. That's who ran me over: my chemistry teacher, Mrs. Claypool. I used to think she was hot and smart—long red hair cascading past her safety goggles as she purred on about isotopes and halogens. But now, honestly, I don't really care for her. You'll pardon my grudge.

Anyhow, now I have a lot of spare time. When I'm not popping in on friends and family (miserable), I hang out at the old Egyptian theater at the end of High Street. You know the one— broken down, boarded up '30s movie palace that looks like it could be a hangout for ghosts? Well guess what? It's a hangout for ghosts.

I don't really get how it works, but it seems to be some sort of way station. People die and if they're moving on—to an after-life, I guess—they walk up the steps in the center of the lobby, looking really happy, and then kind of melt into this Egyptian sphinx mural on the landing. There's lights and tinkly music when that happens—it's pretty cool.

But if they're "unresolved"—that's the term I've come up with—you see 'em kind of floating around the lobby, blinking on and off like lightning bugs. I can't talk to them. At least, I haven't figured out how yet. I recognize a couple of them—they were my dad's patients and just sick with something. But most of 'em are banged up like me. Accident victims.

It's very weird at the Egyptian, but it's kinda nice to have a clubhouse, you know? And it's a stylin' one too: Nile-blue walls with gilt trim and a hieroglyph border, great old movie posters, an ornate box office that looks like a pharaoh's litter. I'm not sure what the Hollywood/Egypt connection is, but who cares? It's fun stuff for a retro-loving guy like me. A glittering refuge. Which I *really, really* need when I get overwhelmed watching my mother stand in my closet, smelling my shirts and crying.

That kind of thing gets to you. In fact, if I really think about my mom falling apart and my brother turning to stone and my dad trying to make desperately cheerful, *normal* conversation with his patients, I just want to rip my heart out. And I don't have a heart anymore. I had one—a heart that beat happily for my family, my girlfriend, my town even. I was a life lottery winner: good, solid start and a promising future. And then... Well, I guess we should get to the story of my death. It's a gripping tale that I wish I could tell my friends. Margo didn't enjoy it, but that's understandable. Here we go:

It was Saturday night, July 1st. Everyone still buzzed on that *yow, summer's here!* vibe. My buds and I were having a cornfield party, which is what you do in Nebraska if you're seventeen on a nice summer night. Pull up the pickup, light the lanterns, crack the brews someone's older brother picked up. Half moon, tunes cranking, sweet smell of new corn—*awesome.*

That night it was me and Ty Cloninger and Jase Phillips and my brother Boyd. Talking guy stuff, leaving the girlfriends at home. (Actually, I'm the only one with a girlfriend. Jase thinks of Grace Pettit as his girlfriend, but it's really just a sad delusion.) It was getting late and Ty started bitching on and on about his summer job, how hard it is to clean the slushie machine at the QuickChek, blah blah snore, and I thought, *I could be making out with my girlfriend right now.* Margo usually watches a movie with her dad on Saturday nights. They're close, her mom died, I get it. But then he goes to bed, which presents an opportunity, and not one to be missed.

Ty had driven and he didn't want to leave yet, so I said screw it, I'll walk back to town. Nice night, right? Why not? Here's why not: you know how they say in driver's ed, "Don't count on other people to pay attention"? It's true, folks. It's true.

I don't know what was happening in that Explorer. Maybe her favorite song from the '90s came on her MP3. Nirvana or Pearl Jam, I'd like to think—something cool, death-worthy. And she was singing with her eyes closed and didn't realize she was veering right. Or maybe she leaned over to smooch her lover, Mr. Hawkins. (My English teacher, remember, and not her husband, Sam Claypool. Oh, the things you find out when you're dead.)

I understand from my female friends that Mr. Hawkins (actually, let's call him Ted. He co-killed me, which I think puts us on a first-name basis) is Carolyn's male hot teacher equivalent. So maybe they were so caught up in their mutual hotitude that they didn't notice a teenager walking by the side of the road. I'll never know. But I *do* know that I saw the headlights and moved over to the far lip of the road. Obviously not far enough.

And they were coming fast, man, *brutally* fast. When they made impact, I actually went up and over the Explorer, which is a large vehicle. And then I'm lying there, broken and *very, very* surprised. Lots of commotion; much freaking out from the hot teachers.

Ted recognized me—he's also my advisor on the school paper—which double-freaked him. He checked for my pulse, screamed for Carolyn to call 911. And she screamed back that she would, but he had to leave first. Which is part of why I really hate her now—it was more important for her lover to disappear than to get me help. Not that it would have mattered, I don't think. You ever see a marionette, with the wooden limbs in pieces on strings? That was me, limp, my blood oozing onto Route 15. Ted cradled my head in his lap, begging: "Stay with me, Hank, you're gonna be okay!" while Carolyn screamed at him to run (despise her). I was *not* gonna be okay, and when he finally realized that, he did run. My journalism mentor, who I actually *really liked*, sprinted into the darkness like a jackrabbit, leaving me broken on the road.

What would the headline be for *that*, Mr. Hawkins? How about, simply, "Trusted Mentor Leaves Protégé to Die." I think that captures it.

The next thing that happened, the last thing really, as moths flitted past the headlights, was that my brain engaged in a slow, somber countdown. An actual countdown:

10... 9... 8... Margo!!!
... 7... 6... 5...
... my little brother and I running through the backyard sprinkler...
... 4... 3... 2...
1

Darkness.

And that's the story of how my clock stopped. How my life was stolen by inattentive lovers. So quick, a seventeen-year-old's plans and dreams, *over*. I had *stuff to do*, man, things to *accomplish!*

All of it, all of me, *gone*, in the heat lightning of a sad summer night.

Anyhow. That's how it ended. And began. After I died, I floated upwards (yeah, that's all true), saw the EMS guys working on me, the cops arriving. That part wasn't bad, once I left my body. A relief from the shock and suffering. I didn't even react when I heard Carolyn tell the cops that I "appeared out of nowhere." (I was walking in front of you on the shoulder!!) At that moment, I didn't care. I just floated up and away over cornfields on a soft July breeze. It was oddly pleasant, in a melancholy way, like an airborne funeral procession. I wafted across town and then down into the theater.

I think I could have left right then. Walked up the stairs at the Egyptian and melted into the sphinx mural. It was very appealing—the beautiful lights and music started up for me.

But I couldn't. I couldn't leave Margo.

So I walked out the theater door (I didn't know how to pop from place to place yet), went over and sat on Margo's porch all night. Waited for her dad to wake her up with the news. I could have gone up to see her reaction, but I didn't. Too awful. Too gut-wrenchingly sad.

I left the party because I wanted to kiss Margo, and now I'll never kiss her again. Never kiss her eyelids, or the mole on her neck, or any of the other lush, sacred places on her body. And that *sucks*.

But at least we can hang out. Lie in the grass on the near bank of the Logan, looking up at the sky through the birch leaves. So I'm holding on to that.

The fact that Margo's the only one who can see and hear me says something on a spiritual level, I think. That says "soulmate" to me, and you can't leave your soulmate behind. Right? So here I am.

I just wish I had a little more to do. One surprising perk: I can play musical instruments now (I never could when I was alive). I just have to think of one and it appears. Actually, it's not so much *thinking* as *feeling*: whatever I feel or the people around me are feeling kind of materializes in my hands in the form of an instrument, and then I start *playing the mood*. Mellow acoustic guitar, angry trumpet, brooding violin. The instruments are no more real than I am—they're part of my Other World—but they're the only things I can touch and it feels good. Expressive.

But even that doesn't really fill the days. I get so bored that sometimes I spy on people I don't really know. I'm a journalist. I'm nosy. I popped into the huddle of a football game, just to see what they talk about, but it was mostly just hilarious confusion. I found out that our school librarian likes to butter her toes and then have her cat lick it off. I did not need to know that.

I've spied on Carolyn and Ted a couple of times—I figure they have it coming. Carolyn got *nothing*, not so much as a slap on her pretty wrist, for killing me. In Nebraska there's no vehicular manslaughter charge unless there's proof that the driver was driving recklessly.

She was! She had to have been! But the police report says I *appeared out of nowhere.* Plus Ty, Jase, and Boyd eventually wandered toward the flashing lights that night and explained my presence to the police. Cornfield party with beer immediately casts me as an oblivious, staggering drunk (which I was *not*). I'm glad I left before they showed up. I'm glad I didn't have to see my little brother find out I was dead. To see a pain so agonizing that the whole of him has calcified now.

Anyhow, that's the final headline on the story of my sudden demise, both legally and in the court of public opinion: *Drunken Teen Lurches in Front of Oncoming Car Driven By Beloved Schoolteacher.* Case closed. Which allows Carolyn Claypool to continue to stride freely through her charmed, devious life.

So I spy on her. And Ted.

I've watched her grading papers in the glossy kitchen of her rich husband's house. I think I've been looking for a tear or two of remorse, a *smidgen* of a dark night of the soul, but no. Nada.

I've watched Ted gliding into his downtown coffee place, charming the baristas. No apparent suffering there either.

I've seen the pair of them feverishly fumbling with zippers and buttons at a *highway motel*, for God's sake. Does it get cheesier than that? (Just to be clear, I pop out before anything truly naughty happens; I'm a principled phantom.)

And here's what I've learned in my investigative travels through the ghostosphere: they're up to something. They occasionally, soberly mention *the accident*, so there's a *little* guilt there, or at the very least *acknowledgement*.

But this is something else.

In the dusky gloom of their room at the Wayfarer, post-sexy time, they talk about *how* they're going to do it, *when* they're going to do it, whatever *it* is. And they get very whispery and dark during these discussions, so I'm pretty sure they're not planning a pep rally.

All I'm saying is, I wouldn't be a bit surprised if Carolyn's husband Sam showed up at the Egyptian sometime soon.

JUNE HUDSPETH'S DIARY:
TUESDAY, SEPT 4

- update LPD website: trash pickup has returned to regular schedule following Labor Day weekend
- another farmer sold out to S.C. Get butts in chairs for town council vote on Willow Grove!
- check FCC regulations viz G.H.'s radio sermons. Over-the-top *crazy!*
- get a read on E.J.'s demeanor
- talk to L.R. again. *No more bumbling.*
- something with Margo. Movies, dinner. I'm here for her.
- resolve Cold Case On

FOUR

MARGO

'm sitting in the school counselor's office with Hank's brother Boyd. We've been meeting for a couple weeks, before school even started. The counselor, Mike, told us at the first meeting that they put us together because "the more connected we are, the better we feel." But honestly, I think it's just efficient. We have the same issue, so why not put us on the recovery train together?

So every Wednesday, Boyd and I have to sit in Mike's office surrounded by peaceful, reassuring pictures and slogans. Sunrise on the beach over the word "hope." "Let go, let God." And one that I think is particularly lame: "When the waves get too high, get a bigger surfboard." It's catchy, but just not that relatable in Nebraska. How about, "When you feel smothered by all the corn, trust God to pull you out" or something.

I actually feel for Counselor Mike, having to paste on his comforting smile all day with all the cutters, druggies, abuse victims. So I talk, just to keep things moving, and because I know Boyd won't. Boyd sits statue-still, everything frozen but one twitchy leg. I wish I could jump up and hug him for about an hour, but I don't want to freak him out more than he already is. He's always been reserved. Even though he's almost six feet tall now and fall-over-yourself handsome, inside he's still that shy kid tailing his very un-shy big brother.

I realize now I've always taken Boyd for granted—a sweet, quiet guy, but somehow just part of the landscape of Hank and his family. But now that it's the two of us in this counseling scenario, I really feel his presence: the anger, the despair, the confusion.

You never know who your fellow survivor is going to be, who's going to stand next to you on the windy plain of grief. Both of you trying to stay upright, both desperate for *normal life* to resume. That's a bond. So yeah, I see Boyd now.

I hear myself blathering on, filling the dead air. At the first meeting, Mike gave us a printout on the stages of grief; I'm kind of riffing off that.

"I think I'm getting past the *shock* and *sleepwalking* feeling and into the *rollercoaster* feeling, you know, up and down, but not too bad."

I want to give Mike enough to sound convincing, like my recovery is *on track*, but not so much color that I set off any mental health alarms.

The whole time I'm talking, I feel like I'm up above my body watching the scene below me. Kind of like Hank, the night he died.

It's all so *false*. I wonder what would happen if I said how I really feel. Like how I felt like my head was going to explode when I ran into Mrs. Claypool this morning. Thank God Delia was with me. Delia—or Delia Chang, PTA (Proud Token Asian), as she calls herself—is my best friend. She and her family are the only Asian Americans in Lazarus; they run the Chinese restaurant. Lazarus is pretty whitey-white, other than the two Mexican families Delia calls "my beloved non-Caucasians." Delia's a hoot.

She and Hank were the riff-masters, always trying to top each other, to see who could make me laugh harder. I'm sure she's been going through her own sorrow since Hank died, but she's pushed it aside to be my rock. *Love* her.

Here's an example of why: we were walking down the hall this morning, and everyone is either pretending not to look at me or coming up and giving me the concerned look/arm touch/ "how are you *doing?*" when suddenly Delia doubles over laughing. Laughs so hard she drops her backpack. I give her a "what the…" look, and she stands back up, whispers, "I'm laughing because I want everyone to think you just said something hilarious, because that's how *fine* and *not a victim* you are." And then *I* start laughing, loving my Deel, and we're walking and laughing so hard we almost bump into Carolyn Claypool.

I don't know who was more freaked, but my money's on her. She just went pale and gape-y, before she remembered who she was supposed to be and put on her teacher face.

"Hey Margo," she said. "Good to see you. How was your summer?" And this is where time slowed down. The words were floating out there between us, too late to take back, alarm bells going off in her eyes—O*h God, why did I say that?* Kids slowing down to watch this new car crash. Delia hovering between us like a nervous boxing ref.

I froze for a moment. I was looking into my boyfriend's killer's eyes. But I *refused* to lose it, not there in the school hallway. I kept my cool. After all, I'm Margo Pierce, the police chief's daughter whose mother was murdered. Whose mother's killer was never found. I've been dragged behind the runaway train of fate; I think I can handle small talk.

"It was okay," I said. "I worked a lot."

Which was true. I worked at the Uptown Boutique all summer, coasting through power surges of shock and pain while arranging peppy window displays. Mannequins in rompers and swimsuits frolicking with a beach ball—an insane contrast to what was going on in my head.

Carolyn looked so grateful for this *normal* reply, I thought she might cry. The universe was restored, motion sped up, we were just teacher and student again.

"*Good.* Good to see you. See you both in class."

And then we moved on, Delia clutching my elbow.

But the surreal-fest wasn't over: my next class was with Mr. Hawkins. He greeted me kindly, but not overly so. A brief hand-clasp and the quick gift of his soulful brown eyes. My guess is that he had run through this moment in his mind. *Don't overdo it, Ted, because* you were not involved.

But then when class started, after all the usual welcome back, here's what we'll be doing, etc., he got serious. Almost *dramatically* serious, casting a look my way, and I thought, *Uh-oh, here it comes. He's going to be The Cool Teacher Who Deals With the Hard Thing.* He said he wanted to read us a poem that might help us with what we'd been feeling this summer. This is the poem, by someone named Rossetti:

Remember me when I am gone away
Gone away far into the silent land
When you can no more hold me by the hand,
Nor I half-turn to go, yet turning to stay

I sat there thinking, *No, no, why are you doing this to me?* But on he went, with a quick flip of his dark, tousled hair. Poet hair; he's perfect for this role. All he needs is a puffy white shirt to replace his Gap neutrals.

Remember me when no more day by day
You tell me of our future that you planned:
Only remember me; you understand
It will be late to counsel then or pray.

Heads turning oh-so-slightly to see how I'm doing. I was boiling, melting and fusing to my chair—*that's* how I was doing.

Yet if you should forget me for awhile

And afterwards remember, do not grieve:
For if the darkness and corruption leave
A vestige of the thoughts that I once had
Better by far you should forget and smile
Then you should remember and be sad.

And then he looked at me, and for just a minute, I saw the guilt in his eyes. Guilt and pain and apology and helplessness and a lot of what I've been feeling. I didn't want to connect with him but I did.

I remember him and Hank working late on the school paper, getting punchy, spit-balling wise-ass stories—"Algebra: Is It Useless or Completely Useless?" Laughing till they cried.

He missed Hank too, I could see it, and this was his stupid English teacher way of expressing it. I could almost forgive...

"What do you think? Is Rossetti right? Forget and smile rather than remember and be sad?" the teacher inquired softly.

And then the Good Students started to chatter, and he called on them, satisfied that he had *handled the situation*, and any connection vanished. My blood was up again.

You were there that night and you don't even have the guts to admit it. You just sit there reading your poem, making the girls swoon at your *depth*. But I know all about you, Professor Charm. You and your married lover, and your creepy radio minister father and how you wake up screaming from nightmares every night. You don't fool me.

I will not play along and *I will not forgive you.* For doing whatever you did in that car that distracted Carolyn and killed Hank and Madolyn. Madolyn was the name I had picked out for the daughter that Hank and I were supposed to have, the future that I planned. The kid who would smile Hank's crinkly smile and chase around after me like I used to chase after my mother and make me whole again.

No, I don't forgive you for taking that away.

Uh-oh. Mike is looking at me. Clearly, he's asked me a question, and I didn't hear it. But that's okay. They expect you to space out during grief counseling.

"I'm sorry," I say. "What?"

"I said it seems like you're right on track with your processing, Margo."

I smile. *Yes.* I'm *right on track.*

"Now, I just have to ask you guys a question. Sorry, but it's required."

I nod: sure. Boyd's still a statue.

"You're not using any drugs or alcohol, are you? You know, to numb the pain?"

I'm just about to say no, no, of course not, when Boyd finally speaks: "Just a speedball to start the day and a fifth of Jack to end it. That's not too much, is it?"

Mike and I freeze. Then I hear Hank laughing. I glance to my right and there he is, feet up on a chair. And I think: he's still here. *Thank God.*

I'm reassured but Mike is not, because he doesn't realize Boyd is giving him a classic James Brothers flip-off.

"I'm sorry," Mike stammers, "but if you're really doing that, I have to…"

"I'm *not.*" Boyd glares at him. "You don't have to write it down. All you have to do is mark me here, because that's all I can give you. Because my recovery is *not* right on track."

With that, he's up and out the door.

Hank and I exchange a look. I want to run after Boyd, tell him, "It's okay; he's still here!" But I don't. Because then my secret would be out and they'd have to go get the big net. So I just sit there, shaking my head for Mike's benefit and ignoring Hank, who's now playing a sad song on an oboe.

On the handout they gave us at the first meeting, on the bottom, after a long explanation of the whole miserable grieving process, it says: "See! You're not going crazy!"

I hope they're right.

JUNE'S DIARY:
THURSDAY, SEPT 6

7:00 tonight
Be concise. Conversational, not confrontational. Courage, remember JoAnn.
Lord be with me.

SIX

HANK

know when someone's about to come over. I can feel it—this
gut feeling—right before someone in town dies. I got it before
that stupid accident on 91: a car trying to avoid a pig smashed
into another car. Sure enough, not long after the crash, both driv-
ers showed up at the theater looking bewildered. A central
casting farmer in overalls and a buzz-cut, and a senior citizen—
glasses half-shattered, Sansabelt pants—getting the Early Bird
Special to Heaven.

I knew it when that farmer out west of town was crushed in a
tractor rollover. (He did *not* look good when he arrived at the
theater. I won't be graphic, but let's just say he no longer needed
two sleeves.) And I can feel it now, except it's worse this time.
Really deep, *queasy*, like it's someone I know. I can feel it when
someone's coming over, and I'm afraid it's my mom.

I'm watching her now, sitting on the end of my bed. It's after dinner, which she didn't eat. She's just sitting there, staring,
hands in her lap. So beautiful, my mom: small and trim with dark
brown hair in a soft wave to her shoulders. But the picture's not

right; the way she's dressed is off. My mom's always been a sharp dresser. She and Margo could talk fashion for days. Even just for around the house, the doctor's wife always looked put together. But since the accident she slouches around in sweats and my dad's t-shirts. She just doesn't care. Today it's a sweatshirt in Drab Gray with Crying-My-Eyes-Out blue sweats. I don't know why this upsets me; it's just clothes. I guess it's just part of the General Unravelling of Mom, and it's *sad*.

But what really worries me is the stillness. For the past two months she's been flapping around like a wounded crow, *raging*, trying to fix this somehow. Sobbing in my father's arms at night in bed, the night table light on, my doctor-father doing his best to soothe her. Going to that lame psychic who told her "Hank wants you to know he's okay."

I didn't tell you anything, *bi-otch,* and there's a lot more than that I want to say. Like *I'm still here, Mom. Two teachers mowed me down, but there's no conspiracy. I'm okay and I want you to move on and be a mom to your other son. I love you, I miss you, and don't spend any more money on psychics!*

Maybe the most painful scene was seeing her kneeling in church on a weekday morning trying to work out a deal with God. Heartbreaking. The bargaining stage, I guess, but it's not going to work. I'm not coming back, Mom. I wish you could hear me.

But she can't, and her eerie stillness tonight is unnerving.

I was the center of my mom's life. Sorry, but there it is. When I was six, she and I went trick-or-treating as the Men in Black, from the movie. Black suits and ties, dark glasses—fun mother/son bad-assery. You might think it would be me and Boyd—we're only a year apart—but no, it was me and Mom. Boyd went as Harry Potter, in my glasses and an eye penciled zig-zag mark on his forehead, tagging behind us. He wasn't even from the same movie.

It was always me and Mom. Robot dancing to the kitchen radio, gleefully knocking over the recipe holder on the butcher-block island in total don't-care mode. Sitting on the couch, mocking out American Idol, sharing a box of Cheez-its (one of the worst things about death: no Cheez-its). And she was front and center of course, clapping like a happy idiot, when I played the narrator in "Our Town" at school. *Mom.*

We thought the same; she has Reporter Brain too, always trying to figure things out. Which is why things got weird, I think. In her mind, I couldn't just die by accident, couldn't just disappear. There had to be a reason.

A month ago I popped in and saw my parents having a standoff in the living room. My dad hanging his head, leaning on the fireplace mantel for support, repeating, "No, Emmie, *no.*" My mom, wild-eyed, blazing a trail around the living room: loveseat to overstuffed bookcase, then around the back of the sofa, back to the coffee table. All the while insisting that I must have *had something* on Carolyn, and she must have known I did. That she saw an opportunity that summer night and hit me on purpose. "Hank was a *newspaperman*, Orrin!" she kept saying to my dad. "He found things out!"

A newspaperman. I was editor of the school paper, which isn't even on paper.

So then it's the three of us standing in a triangle, my mom frothing out this intrigue—*"She cannot be allowed to get away with this!"*—my dad swaying back and forth like he's made of paper, me arguing with thin air: "It was an *accident*, Mom! Just a stupid accident! I didn't have anything on Carolyn Claypool!"

I do now, of course, but that's after the fact. Here's the latest: I was hanging out after school the other day, waiting for Margo to get out of yearbook, when I saw Carolyn slither into Ted's classroom. He was sitting at his desk, grading papers. Dark hair flopping forward, focused. Not constantly anguished, as I would like him to be. Anyhow, Carolyn sidles (that's the only word for it) over and plops onto his lap, right there on a high school afternoon. Then she grabs his head with both hands and plants a big wet one on his lips. And I mean, this was motel kissing, not an excusable school day love peck. He reciprocates for a minute, then pushes her away.

"No," he tells her. "*Not here*." She goes back in for more, eyes a little swimmy—the woman's clearly going slightly bonky—but he stops her.

"I *miss* you," she whispers.

"I know," he says. "But," hands on her shoulders, "you have *got* to get it together, Carolyn, or it won't work. *Nothing we planned will work.*" She nods, leans on him.

Don't tell me there's not a story there (yes, Mom, I am a newspaperman, I guess). I am hot on the trail of these two, but I don't have much yet. Margo says I shouldn't spy on them—"have a little ghostly dignity" is what she actually she said—but I can't help it. I'm curious. I have a lot of time to kill, and honestly, a bit of a vendetta.

SEVEN

MARGO

"Five letter word," Dad says. We've just sat down in our usual booth at Marcy's Diner. Dinner out at Marcy's, a first-week-of-school tradition.

I groan, then remind him that you can't really play this game with only two people. At this, his eyes twinkle, he leans in. "You're just scared you can't solve my word," he says. He knows this'll get me.

"E?" I ask.

"Nope," he replies, pleased.

"A?" He shakes his head.

We almost never use words with E or A in them, but they're the most common letters so you have to get them out of the way. We've been playing this game since I was little, when Mom invented it. As a vocab booster probably—my mom was big on language skills. She'd pick easy words when Dad and I were the guessers, and Dad would let me win after a big show of struggling to beat me. And later, after Mom died, we'd play with

Hank, round after round of ferocious competition. No more letting anyone win. Five Letter Word goes way back with us.

"I?" I inquire.

"Third letter."

"Hmm," I say. "The old I-in-the-middle."

Dad grins. It's so lame but it's so *us* that it's also kinda great.

I'm distracted by the new décor at Marcy's. The owner, Al Nordgren, re-did the place over the summer. The booths and chair backs are aqua blue and so are the walls, broken up by panels of marbled mirrors. It's nice, sort of, nicer than it was, but there's something jarring about the color. I think maybe we're just not aqua blue people here in northeast Nebraska. Miami Beach, maybe, or Malibu. Those are your aqua bluers.

"Third letter I," Dad repeats, bringing me back.

"S?" I ask.

"Yes!" he declares, delighted. "First letter." Even though I'm sixteen now and the only player, he still wants me to win.

"S blank I blank blank," I murmur, trying to act as into it as he is. It's sweet that he still wants his kid to win. Maybe even more this year.

We're interrupted by the arrival of Lulu, the forties-ish waitress. We greet her, then Dad asks, with a wink: "What are the specials tonight, Lulu?"

There are never specials at Marcy's. Just the regular menu. But Lulu plays along.

"Oh, now, you know everything on that menu's special, Chief," Lulu says, her smile revealing one chipped front tooth. All the single women in town flirt with my dad. It used to bother me, but I'm over it.

Dad starts to order a meaty-cheesy-gloppy dinner but I interrupt, ordering for him.

"He'll have the steak, lean and well-done, and the dinner salad."

Dad sighs, allowing this, though he can't help but add, "But can you substitute bacon for the cucumbers?"

After I head this off and Lulu leaves, we continue the game. I know his word. He's used it before.

"I don't suppose this word would've been used by, say, the Grinch, would it?"

Which allows him to sing, over-loud, *"Stink! Stank! Stunk!"*

This was a howler when I was six. I'm mildly embarrassed but also kinda love it. We may be a family of two now, but the old traditions, the dumb gags, and the deep love that go with them carry on.

I settle in and wait for my tuna melt.

EIGHT

HANK

've been looking at my mom sitting on her bed for forty-two minutes. Both of us motionless. It's both sad and fascinating. Because when, in life, do you ever stop and really look at your mom? You always just kind of expect her to be *there*, right? No need to *study* her.

But in this one-sided staring contest, I'm noticing things: her shoulders, rounder than they used to be. Wisps of gray in her hair, a sallow cast to her face. Her eyebrows growing in at a jagged cant; I guess she stopped plucking them.

But her sea-green eyes are still alert and intelligent, which tells me she's in there somewhere, trying to sort herself out. She just needs help.

If I were alive, I could get her to laugh again. I could bring her back.

But if I were alive, she wouldn't be like this. The stricken statue.

I hear footsteps on the stairs; Mom doesn't move. Boyd appears in the doorway. Most of the time these days he's the Stone

Man, not looking at Mom or anyone else. But deep down he's a scared kid, I can tell. He wants her back and I want her back for him. Now he just hovers in the doorway, uncertain.

"*Come in*, Boyd," I say out loud. "*Sit* with her. She needs you."

He can't hear me, I know that, but he comes in. Just stands there. "Hey" is all he can manage. Not much, but I'll take it. Better than I can do.

Mom's reaction times have slowed down, like the rest of her. After a full minute passes, she looks up at him. "Oh hi, honey." Emotionless.

Come on, Boyd. Put an arm around her, tell her it'll be okay. Come on, you useless piece of...

No. It's not Boyd's fault he can't cheer her up. They just don't have the same connection we had. The other night she blew up at him for not knowing the rules to backgammon. That was our game. She freaked on him for not being me. Boyd just went to his room, lay on his bed, and stared at the ceiling. Sudden death's a bitch.

"Did you know it's Back-to-School Night?" he says.

She looks at him. Blinks. "Oh. Is that tonight?"

"Yeah, it already started, but I'm sure it's still going. I'll take you over if you want." All right, Boyd. *My man.*

But Mom doesn't respond. Nothing.

Boyd blunders on, stuttering, "Thought it might be good... Get out, see people... talk to my teachers..."

Boyd is six feet tall, looks like a young movie star in jeans and a muscle tee, but he's just freakin' blabbering.

And yet, miraculously, a little life comes into Mom's face. She starts to nod. "Yes. *Yes.* Maybe I will."

Boyd breathes for the first time since he came in. "That's great, Mom. I'll take you over."

She nods again, rolling the idea around. Finally: "Okay."

And now she actually smiles, which feels like a Twins home run in post-season extra innings. *Go Boyd.* He smiles back and walks out, ten pounds lighter. Mom sits there thinking for a few minutes. The smile disappears; her face turns dark. *Determined,* suddenly. She gets up, walks into her bedroom. Gets a black purse out of her closet. Then crosses to my dad's nightstand. Opens the top drawer. Takes out a small pistol and puts it in her purse. My gut clenches with that strong feeling again. *Someone's coming over tonight.*

MARGO

'm t-shirt girl at Back-to-School Night. We're in the cafeteria, Delia's in charge of refreshments. I'm selling Lazarus High t-shirts, sweatpants, coffee mugs, etc. Anything maroon and silver that'll raise funds for the school.

There's really nothing for Delia to do at the snack table; the mounds of homemade brownies, cookies, and lemon bars are already laid out, the cider already poured. So she's hanging at my table, keeping me entertained.

The presentations are over so parents and teachers are just milling around, snacking and chatting. Delia can do the voices of most of the teachers and even some of the parents and she's improv-ing Onion-style versions of their conversations. Dressed (ironically, of course) as the ultimate team spirit girl in maroon tights and a silver sweater, Delia's my favorite local comedian. She has me laughing till my face hurts. In a good way.

It's nice. We've all gotten through the first three days of school post Summer-of-Hank, and now here we are in a good ol' Lazarus world of mom-made brownies. LHS banner over the little stage, Principal Steffens pontificating to semi-interested parents. A couple of overly perky cheerleaders chirping to a mom about the joys of butt-flashing flips, or whatever it is cheerleaders talk about. Back to school, back to normal.

Across the room I see Carolyn Claypool wrangling an overly attentive dad. She really is our red carpet-ready fashion star, tonight in a form-fitting coral dress that sets off her coppery hair. The dad is nervous, over-talking, shifting from foot to foot like a teenager asking his dream girl to prom. Carolyn's laughing, going with it, clearly glad to just be the Hot Chem Teacher again, not the Tragically Reckless Driver.

I see her steal a glance at Ted, who winks back. Then looks nervously over at Carolyn's husband Sam, who's schmoozing parents by the snack table. Oh Ted, you handsome weenie, you.

Sam catches my eye and starts heading our way. He's a stout little Napoleon in an expensive gray suit (no one else wears suits to this, it's just Back-to-School Night, you big show-off). So now I'll have to make conversation with the guy my dad calls The Oil Slick.

"Margo! Delia!" Sam says as he reaches us. Like any good salesman, he's got all the names down. "Two of Lazarus's loveliest."

Under the table, a kick from Delia.

"Hi Mr. Claypool."

"What have we got here? I can always use a good sweatshirt."

"We're all out of extra-large," Delia blurts. I give her a look but she doesn't care.

Sam looks at her, unfazed. "Delia Chang. Your parents run the Dragon House, right?"

"Yes, sir."

"You all still living up top? In that little apartment?"

I know where he's going with this and it annoys me. I've always loved Delia's family's apartment. It just looks so different from anyone else's house; so eclectic and alluring to the senses. In the living room, a classic Chinese framed print of a misty mountainside flanked by Chinese lettering faces off with a print of Degas' dancers on the opposite wall. A glossy gold six-paneled room divider with a heron print sits just beyond a mid-century modern blue couch. The soft sheen of dark rosewood furniture, the gentle song of brass windchimes, the smell of Cantonese cooking floating up from the restaurant below—an aroma so sweet and dreamy you just tingle. Whenever I see a New Mexico license plate, I think of Delia's apartment: the Land of Enchantment.

"Yes," she tells Sam, "we're still there."

"Must be a little tight up there, eh? You, your parents, and your brother."

"We like it," Delia replies evenly.

"Well," says Sam, and here comes the shark look, the glint in the eye, "you tell your parents I'm gonna have a beautiful three-bedroom detached house with their name on it over at Willow Grove. Backyard, two bathrooms, laundry room. They can use that old apartment for storage space for the restaurant."

Sam doesn't know who he's dealing with. Delia smiles sweetly. "But Mr. Claypool, Willow Grove isn't approved yet, is it? Don't you still have to get it past the town council?"

Now the glint in Sam's eyes disappears, replaced by steel.

"Oh, it'll pass," he says. "Don't you worry about that. Just tell your parents, okay? Tell 'em to come see me."

Before Delia can answer, my dad's there, swooping in like Batman. He's a head taller than Sam; only Sam's money evens the power balance.

"Whatcha up to, Sam? Trying to sling property that doesn't exist yet? And to a teenager, no less."

Here we go. Sam and my dad have been going at it like this since high school. They were both major players back in their LHS days: Dad was football captain; Sam was student council president. And they both wanted the same girl: my mom. That's the root of this endless battle. Sam chased my mother relentlessly, but she picked Dad. And so it drags on, long after my mom's death.

Sam looks at my Dad, his eyes shining black.

"Face it, Roy. Willow's going to happen. Everything's in order, plus this community needs affordable housing."

"Really? Seems to me we've got plenty of affordable housing. And I haven't noticed a big population influx. People swarming in trying to capitalize on all the career opportunities at the Hy-Vee."

One point, Roy. At my side, I can feel Delia enjoying this.

"You might be surprised. Lazarus is headed for a major upswing."

"Oh, I'm sure you've got some kind of racket going. You always do. But until there's really a need for it, I'm gonna see that you don't displace all these farmers you're trying to boot out. They've worked too hard to be snake-oiled out of their land."

The room just got a little hotter. Delia grabs a cookie, wrapped up in the action.

Sam's eyes are ice now. After a long minute, they start to sparkle. He turns to me. "I was just noticing what a fine young thing Margo's getting to be. She's got her mother's shape. Everything in the right places."

I feel my mouth falling open and have to force it shut. Are you kidding me?! What is he *doing?*

Sam pauses, then turns it up a notch, leering: "Mm-*mmm.* If I was twenty years younger, I'd be on that like white on rice."

Dad takes a step towards Sam, his face flushing crimson. But his voice is soft thunder: "I know what you're trying to do, Sam. You want me to hit you so you can insist on my removal to the town council. But I won't do it. I want to stay in uniform so I can keep after your Ralph Laurened ass every crooked step you take. And make no mistake, I will stop your little shanty town cold."

They're eye to eye, hothead to hothead. Well, Sam has to look upwards to face Dad, but his crazy-competitive zeal seems to give him an extra lift.

I should defuse this somehow. My mother would've known just the right calming thing to say. But I don't.

Finally, Sam breaks the standoff with a smile. "Nice to talking to you, Roy. I think I'll get some cider."

And he's off, my dad's glare following him. Then Dad remembers us and coughs, looks down, embarrassed. Pulls at his shirt cuffs. "I'm sorry you girls had to hear that."

I want to tell him it's okay, everything's okay, just *calm down*, Dad. I don't like it when he gets hot like that. Dr. James said he's got to watch his blood pressure.

I'm trying to think of the perfect thing to say when suddenly Hank appears at Dad's side, looking agitated.

Oh *come on*. Not now, Hank.

Dad's still pulling himself together, fumbling for words. "Sam Claypool's just a jerk. Always has been."

"Margo," Hank says. *"Margo!"*

I ignore him. Dad needs me, needs to know I'm okay, and I will *not* be distracted.

"There's no excuse," he mutters. "No excuse for that kind of..."

"Margo!!" Hank's begging now, trying to grab my arm, though he knows his hand will just pass through me. "I need your help! My mom's got a gun in her purse. I think she's going to shoot Carolyn Claypool!"

What?! I stare right at him for a second. My dad notices; he doesn't miss a thing.

I look over: there's Hank's mom, stalking unsteadily towards Mrs. Claypool. Dressed randomly in sweats and sneakers and her stylish single-breasted camel coat. And yes, she's clutching a little black purse. *Oh crap.*

I fix Dad with a look that I hope conveys instant reassurance. "It's okay, Dad. I know Sam—he doesn't bother me." Then lamely: "Oh geez, someone left the outside door open."

And then I'm off, ricocheting across the room between parent clusters. Smiling a crazed smile—"Excuse me!"—trying to get through the crowd.

Hank's at my side. I whisper to him: "How do you know?"

"I *saw* her!" Hank spouts. "It's the pistol Dad keeps in his nightstand. Plus I can *feel* it, Marg. Someone in town's going to die tonight!"

Kathy Quinn's mom plants herself in front of me, and she is not a small woman. With her curled-under hair, print dress, and sensible shoes, she's full-on old-school Nebraska.

"Margo!" She beams, wrapping me up in her meaty arms. "How *are* you, sweetheart?"

Over her shoulder, Hank pleads with me. Emmie is getting close to Carolyn, who has her back turned.

I try to pull away, but Mama Quinn's embrace is a vise. She takes hold of my shoulders, fixes me with a look. "I've been thinking about you all summer, honey. *Such* a shame. How are you getting along?"

She smells like baby powder and the expression on her face is genuinely, touchingly concerned. Suddenly I'd like to stop, find a big chair, and climb into her lap. Just cry while she hugs me and says nice, mom-ish things.

But over her shoulder I see Emmie James reaching into her purse.

I dive under Mrs. Quinn's arm and lunge for Emmie's arm. *Got her.*

She turns and stares at me, shocked. It's like a switch has been thrown. A moment of hesitation and then suddenly it's our private world, Emmie's and mine. I can see my own feelings in her gray-green eyes. It's like there's some kind of dark lightning between us; the history and shared pain ricochet back and forth. Her arm relaxes, falls to her side.

"Tell her to go home," whispers Hank, but I've got this.

"It's too much, isn't it?" I tell her gently. "All this."

She looks at me, then slowly nods. *Yes. It's all too much.*

Joined by our eyes, I try to fill her up with my strength. I'm a rock in the ocean; she's a wave breaking against me. It's working. She's relaxing, her shoulders drop an inch. She's emerging out of the darkness, just a little.

Boyd joins us. "What's going on?" That little boy voice, scared.

"Your mom's just a little overwhelmed," I tell him. "I think you should take her home."

"I'm sorry," he bleats. Upset, breathing hard. He's put a white dress shirt on, which strikes me as achingly sweet in the middle of this madness. He's trying to be a man for his mother, but when he speaks it's with the frightened squeak of a little boy. "I thought it would be good for her…"

"Don't be sorry," I say, looking at him now. "You had the right idea. She's just going through a rough patch."

I've broken eye contact with Emmie, and now she's floating out to sea. When I look back, I see the dark look is back, the tremble. She's looking around, sees people are staring at her. She spots Carolyn.

A ferocious sneer explodes across her face. She lurches forward, hand on her purse.

Slow motion again; I can't seem to move fast enough.

She comes face-to-face with Carolyn, whose cocktail party prettiness drains right out of her.

I can't get there in time. The whole room is holding its breath; our pleasant maroon-and- silver snow globe seems right on the brink of shattering.

But after a brief moment, Emmie turns and walks in the other direction. Then slowly breaks into a trot. And before Boyd, Hank, or I can process what's happening, she's out the open door. Gone.

TEN

HANK

can't fly. I can't even hover, not since the night I died. I can pop over to other places, but that's about it. I can't locate missing people. So my mom has disappeared into the night and I can't find her.

I pop in at home: dirty dishes in the kitchen sink, living room empty, my parents' pale blue bedroom a silent tomb. No Mom.

I can hear my dad in the shower. I wish I could get him out in his car searching, but he can't hear me. So that's out.

I try popping in on my mom's best friend, Sue Cloninger, but Mrs. Cloninger's at Back-to-School Night, of course. Ty Cloninger and his dad are in the den watching some sitcom, Kelly's in the kitchen on her laptop. No help.

I pop into the center of town: nothing, no one on the streets. I can see Al Nordgren cleaning up, getting ready to close Marcy's for the night. I pop into the restaurant; no one's there but Al, wiping down tables. He's got classic rock on, Led Zeppelin, which is cooler than I would expect from hard-working, long-faced, Swedish-American Al. But I don't have time to ponder that; I gotta find Mom.

Out in the street, no more clues, just the town's only stoplight, blinking yellow.

But there is one other light on, in the police station. Out of pure desperation, I pop in there.

At first, I think she's just sleeping. June Hudspeth, Chief Roy's secretary, in her chair at her desk, like always. Her head is hanging backwards, her arms dangle at her sides.

She's wearing a patterned blouse, big magenta flowers, so at first I don't see the stain. But then that feeling kicks in: *I know dead and this is dead.*

I'm paralyzed. It's beyond surreal: me hanging there, a ghost, June's body seated in front of me, lifeless. *I should check for her at the theater,* I think vaguely, but I can't move.

The door opens: it's Chief Roy. "June?" he booms. "What're you still doing..."

He trails off. The chief of police, sizing up the situation in two seconds. Then softly, desperately: *"June?"* He crosses to her, checks her pulse. Then just stands there, staring. A big, tough guy, utterly poleaxed with disbelief.

"I'm so sorry," I say out loud. "I just got here, I didn't see what... I wish I could have..." I'm babbling and he can't hear me anyway, so I stop.

Who would kill June Hudspeth? *June Hudspeth,* Chief Roy's trusty sidekick. Gray-flecked brown hair, sharp eyes behind wire-rimmed glasses. Funny, oddly kinda sexy for sixty years old. Never married, no kids. Lived to support Chief Roy—you could tell.

One thing you could count on in Lazarus, June Hudspeth would always be at her desk, keeping an eye on things. And now...

I realize that Chief Roy's breathing heavily. Too heavily. He bends over, steadying himself on June's desk. Grabs his left shoulder. Then slumps slowly to the ground.

"Roy!" I scream. *No, no, no, not this!* Margo can't take this! I stand over him, helpless.

That's when it hits me: maybe this is why the feeling was so intense. Maybe *two* souls are crossing over tonight.

ELEVEN

MARGO

I've been dozing. After three or four hours of breathing in and out to the rhythm of the machine that's keeping my father alive, as if I was powering it, I gave in to sleep. Officially, visitors aren't allowed to stay this long in the ICU, but Dad's Dad and I'm me, so here I am in the boxy chair at his bedside.

My eyes slit open then closed, each time irritated by something glittery across the room. A couple of years ago the county hospital was completely re-modelled, thanks to an Omaha benefactor with fond memories of his prairie boyhood. They used this glittery tile throughout the hospital—silver, gold, amber—that was meant to be upscale and cheerful, I think. But its golden twinkle reminds me of the Gates of Heaven and that pisses me off. We're not ready for that yet, thank you. I close my eyes.

At least I made it to the hospital this time. With my mom and Hank, there was no need.

Delia and her parents have gone home. They were so sweet, so worried, but their tight little unit made me feel like an orphan already.

Lance Ritter, my dad's deputy, is sleeping in the waiting room. He wears an LPD badge, but he's useless in a crisis. At twenty-eight he's just a big galoofy kid; slight with a shock of reddish-brown hair the same color as his freckles, he actually looks like an arrested adolescent. He was like Dad and June's adopted child, the stray they were helping along. I know he's devastated by June's death and upset about Dad, but he's not family, and it bugged me that I had to keep reassuring *him* all night.

Dr. James, Hank's dad, was here too, conferring with the doctors. He's a good man, but he's gone past his suffering limit. It was hard to see him so pale and shaky; he's usually the wise, kind Comforter-in-Chief. But tonight he was struggling to stand tall, be a physician. I'm glad he left.

I sent my dad out to look for Emmie after she left last night. He knew it was serious, he saw it in my eyes. I asked him to go and he just went. The event broke up pretty quickly after that. It was like people sensed that the back-to-normal mood had shifted with Emmie's meltdown. It felt like a group shudder, a bracing reminder of The Trouble. It was time to go home.

Delia and I were clearing up by the time Hank popped in to tell me about June and Dad. I started gasping like a dying fish and I couldn't tell Delia why. *Process and react*, I kept telling myself, cop-style. *Come on, Margo!*

And then I saw him: Riley Kagan, just leaving the cafeteria with his wife. The head of the Rescue Squad; ginger-haired, reliable Riley. Thank you, God, forever that Riley Kagan was the last to leave Back-to-School Night.

When we got down there, Riley handled everything. We were moving at two different speeds: he called the hospital, called Lance, got the paddles going. Quickly grasped that June was gone and focused all his attention on Dad. I just gaped.

It was awful to see Dad's big chest spasming up and down under the paddles. Just so *wrong*: Chief Roy, who helps everyone else, so helpless. Being loaded into the ambulance, oblivious. Efficient EMTs racing about their business. And me: cool, together Margo, saucer-eyed in the blinking red lights.

Hank was with me, at the station and in the ambulance. My best friend, bumping along on this wild ride with me. But I didn't want him there. He was still Hank, *my* Hank, but he was a ghost and I just couldn't deal with him while I was fighting for my father's life.

The doctors were waiting at the hospital's ambulance bay, grim-faced. Everyone smacked by the gravity of Roy Pierce having fallen. No time to ponder the cause, the fact that the sight of his murdered secretary had stopped my dad's heart.

June Hudspeth. The most solid single entity in Lazarus, *gone*. She was never motherly exactly, although she tried to be after my mom died. More like an aunt. Or a hard, kind, Nebraskan guardian angel, taking care of everything, practically carrying us on her back in the early days after the murder. Making meals, fielding calls, sleeping on our couch, just in case. Pensive, worried but so strong, so protective of us.

I can't let go of her; this woman is fully lodged in my heart.

At the hospital, they were helping my dad better than I could, so I finally had time to think of June. And my main thought was *I will avenge her*. I will figure out who on earth wanted to kill her, and I will bring them to justice. She would expect it of me. Most people think I'm overly responsible for my age, that I take on too much. But June knew she and I were made of the same stuff; she would believe I could handle it. So I will.

It was a long night of confusion interrupted by machine *bloops*. Near dawn, a dream. My mom and I were shoe shopping at Fabulous Footwear downtown. She was kneeling before me, her black coffee hair falling across her face, easing a taupe slip-on shoe on to my foot. Telling me something, but I couldn't hear what. I kept leaning closer; I really wanted to hear, but I couldn't.

I shook awake to the reminder of the breathing machine, the glint of the Gates of Heaven. Then back to sleep, another dream. I was still in the shoe store but Mom was outside now. Standing on the sidewalk with my dad. Laughing, touching his arm. The dark-haired beauty and the football star. I felt an exquisite rush of recognition, pride, and love for my parents. But I couldn't get to them. I tried but I was locked in. I could only watch them through the glass door.

I could only watch them as they walked, hand in hand, down the street away from me.

TWELVE

HANK

wrestled a man back to life. My former future father-in-law. I didn't know I could do it, but I did.

After I popped over to the cafeteria to tell Margo about her dad, I went back to the police station. I knew June was gone, but Roy was still alive. But just barely; his breath was slow, hoarse, noisy, like chains dragged across asphalt.

I knelt next to him, tried to put my hands on his chest but they went right through. As I've said, if he was a netherworld tuba, I could touch him. But he wasn't.

He was practically motionless, rationing his breath, I think. The expression on his face was *startled*—not by June's death anymore, I don't think, but by his own lack of strength.

I had always felt like a pantywaist next to Roy. I mean, the guy is *strong*. One time he asked me to help him move an old playground set that Margo didn't use anymore. He was donating it to a daycare center.

The idea was that he and I would lift the thing up and put it on a flatbed. I looked at the playset and thought, *This is not hap-*

pening. It had a wooden frame supporting two swings, a monkey bar and climbing wall. *Heavy*. I was just about to say, Roy, we need more guys for this, when he lifted his end all the way up, effortlessly, like Superman.

I couldn't even budge my end. And I put everything into it, not wanting to be Scrawny Writer Boy; I was straining, grunting, muscles were popping. *Nothing*. When Roy finally put his end down and got on the phone, I couldn't tell if he was more disappointed or amused. Probably both.

And now here he was, on the floor of his office, all that strength gone. I could see the fear in his eyes; his fists were clenching, then unclenching. As far as he knew, no one was coming to help him.

I talked to him: "That's it, Roy, just keep breathing, in and out. They're *coming*, Roy, I swear."

Then he did the worst thing he could do: He closed his eyes. He *relaxed*. He was giving in.

I stared at him, thinking, *Crap, crap, crap. No, Roy! Hold on!*

And then I saw something strange: a kind of misty gray shadow of Roy starting to float upwards. He was leaving his body. I think you would have to be on the other side, on my side of death, to see it. But I was and I knew.

I just yelled *"No!!!"* and threw myself on top of him. Trying to push his spirit back into his body. I didn't know what else to do. And that's when the truly weird part started: his spirit wanted to leave and I was restraining it. I couldn't touch Roy, but I could touch his spirit, and I was not going to let it move on.

It was intense: Roy's spirit was strong like Roy, and I could feel its rage at being held back. But it was confused: it didn't know the rules of this other realm yet and I did. We were eye to eye, me on top of Roy's spirit self as it flailed around, looking for a way out. It had these wild, new silvery spirit eyes, equal parts rage and anguish.

Finally I gathered all the strength I had, stared at him and yelled, *"You are not leaving yet!"* and pushed down as hard as I could. My arms and legs on his, my meager chest pummeling his expansive one downwards. I got him back in, but I could still see those spirit eyes. Unsure, resisting.

Then a car door slammed. Then footsteps, the door opening. And then the spirit eyes were gone. Roy was just a dying man on the floor of his office again.

A switch from spirit restraining to life saving as the EMTs electro-paddled Roy's heart back to normal. I had this odd thought that Riley Kagan was kind of like Jesus restoring life to the stricken. A Jesus in casual-dad khakis teaching his blue-uniformed disciples Intro to Miracles. Things get pretty spiritual when you watch someone get pulled back from the edge of the abyss. I kinda wondered what Riley could have done for me if he'd been there on Route 15 right after the crash. But he wasn't. So.

I didn't have time to really think about what had happened with me and Roy until I was riding in the ambulance with Margo. I looked at Roy, hooked up to life support, safe in the hands of modern medicine for now. And I thought, *Maybe I'm strong after all.* In life, I couldn't lift the damn swing set, but maybe I'm the Jean-Claude Van Damme of ghosts.

I looked over at Margo but she didn't look back. I thought she was in shock—pale, hunched, staring dully at her father. But later in the ICU, when she was clearly refusing to look at me, I realized she didn't want me there. This was between her and her dad.

So I checked out the waiting room. Delia Chang was there with her parents, Zhen and Wei, who I mostly know as the gracious hosts of the Dragon House. I saw such heartfelt concern in their eyes I wanted to hug them. If things go south with Roy, I know they would take Margo in in a second. Love her back to life. Good, good people, the Changs.

By way of contrast, Jughead Lance occupies the next waiting room seat (cartoon Jughead, not the cool TV one). He has
this dopey "I hope nothing really bad happens" expression on his
face. Ridiculous that he's the Veep to Roy's President of Police
Work.

And then there's my dad, Dr. Orrin James. Conferring with
the staff, discussing Roy's medical condition. In a strange way,
on this Night From Hell, this was the hardest thing of all. Watching my dad trying to keep it together, be an authority figure,
when he was clearly not up to it. My dad, the doctor from the
Norman Rockwell painting, now trembling with stress. His son
lost, his wife lost in a different way, his best friend barely alive
in the next room. My dad was made for healing and laughter and
family and backyard games of catch, not this crap.

If only, I thought, *if only* he had my mother to lean on right
now. My strong, funny, kitchen-dancing mother. And suddenly,
thinking of dancing in the kitchen with her—so in sync, the Hank
and Emmie Show—I knew where she was. So I popped over
there.

It was dark but I could see her shape, lying there in her coat.
Curled into a C, one hand stretched out on flat stone. It was cold,
too cold for a mortal to be outside. I couldn't put a blanket over
her, couldn't comfort her. All I could do was sit with her while
she slept on my grave.

THIRTEEN

MARGO

All night long my brain's been chugging along like a freight train: *my father might die, my father might die, my father might die*. But as morning light glows through the ICU curtains, my brain train stops at a new thought: June *did* die. *That's* what I need to focus on.

For someone I saw nearly every day, I know very little about June. She came to work for my dad before I was born. Before that... another office job? Different police work? No idea.

I know she was religious, a churchgoer. Big Huskers fan. Dressed simply, usually a white button-down, tan skirt, graying hair pulled back. Her only big sartorial flourish was a little Indian turquoise jewelry sometimes in summer. Great laugh when you got her going. But that's about it: no family or geographical history. As far as I know, she sprang full-grown from the plains of Nebraska, ready to assist my dad.

She didn't talk about herself; her attention was always focused outward. It was almost like a magic trick how she always knew what was going on in town. Obviously, she knew more than someone wanted her to know, but I have absolutely no idea who that someone could be. But I do know someone who had a gun in her purse last night.

Hank appears next to me. "Any change?"

I shake my head. We sit in silence for a minute, then he offers: "I found my mom. She slept on my grave last night. She just woke up and went home."

"Is she okay?"

Hank just shrugs.

"Hank," I say, trying not to sound too cop-ish, "I need to talk to her."

Hank narrows his eyes at me. He knows me too well. "Why?"

"Because June was shot last night."

"And?"

I shrug a don't-make-me-spell-it-out shrug, which clearly pisses him off.

"Why on earth would my mom want to kill June Hudspeth? They're *friends*. June came to visit her after I died, sat with her, hugged her. It makes no sense."

I let this hang a minute before I say, "Still. I'll need to do a ballistics check on her gun."

Hank's fuming, leaning in. "Oh, so you're CSI now? Who put you in charge of this investigation?"

"Who else is gonna do it? *Lance?*"

"A *ballistics check*," he sneers. "Like you have the faintest idea how to do that."

"I'll figure it out."

"Margo, my mother did not kill June. That's *insane.*"

"Well, honestly, your mom didn't look entirely sane last night."

"You *know* her," Hank pleads. "She would never do anything like that."

My response is heavily obvious: "Then why did she have a gun?"

Silence. I can almost feel the weight of the situation in the room. We're trying to solve a problem that's way over our heads, and one of us isn't even alive.

One of us isn't even alive.

That's when it hits me: Hank can do something no one else can do. I turn to him, urgent. "Have you checked at the theater? To see if June's there?"

"No, I've been worried about you and my mom," he says.

"Well I don't need you to worry about me. *Get over there.* You're the only one who can ask her who killed her!"

Hank nods, pops out just as a male orderly comes in. Tall, African American, a look of concern re: my yelling.

"Everything okay?" he inquires.

"Yeah, sorry," I bluff. "I'll turn off my phone." I hold it up and click it off, just for emphasis.

The orderly blinks at me. "There's no phone service in here."

"All the more reason to turn it off!" I note cheerily, gathering my things. From the look on his face, it occurs to me that maybe I shouldn't be making the call about who's sane and who's not.

FOURTEEN

HANK

The theater's empty. No confused, hovering spirits. No June. But something's different: I hear a sound. Muffled, like it's in another room. I move toward it until the sound becomes clearer. It's running water. And it's coming from inside the ladies' room.

I open the door. The interior is more Egyptian kitsch/cool: pinkish terra-cotta tiles with a Cleopatra-themed border. But there's no time to appreciate it: the central element in the room is an older woman with her back to me. She's wearing a slip, black skirt, stockings and shoes, and she's washing something out in the sink. The strange thing is, she looks like a real woman. Not translucent or twinkling like the spirits around here usually are.

"Hello?" I say. The woman turns, peers at me through wire-rimmed glasses. It's June.

"Hank?" She scowls. "You do know you're in the ladies' room, right?"

"Yeah, sorry..." I say, my mind blown. "But... you're supposed to be..."

She turns back to her cleaning, frowning.

"I got some kind of awful stain on my blouse. Can't seem to get it out."

Ohh, I realize. She doesn't know she's dead. That's why she's coming in so clearly. She's holding on to her life spirit.

"It's blood," I tell her.

She looks up at me. Puzzled. "*Blood?* How would I have gotten a big blood stain on my blouse?"

I try to tell her gently: "You were shot. Last night, at the police station."

Her arms drop to her sides. She looks at herself in the mirror, more baffled than shocked. "*Shot...*" she murmurs.

She starts to shimmer a bit, remembering. Then pushes it away. "Well, that's just ridiculous," she says. "I wasn't *shot*."

I move closer to her, trying to maintain the same calm tone. "June. I need you to remember who came into the police station last night."

"Last night," she frets. "I don't recall anyone..."

"Someone came in," I continue. "And pulled a gun on you. Who was it, June?"

She shakes her head, goes back to her scrubbing. "I have to get this stain out. Do you mind? This is the *ladies'* room."

"Was it my mother, June? Was it Emmie James?"

She looks at me, blinks. Fades out a little, then back in. Then finally says: "Balsamic dressing. From lunch. I had a salad. I'll bet that's what it is."

She turns determinedly back to her washing.

She's not ready yet. So I'll wait.

MARGO

was an idiot to think I could slip into the police station unnoticed. There's a crowd of gawkers gathered, just like when my mom died. Shopkeepers, retirees, even some kids skipping school, like me. What do they think they're going to see? I'll never understand the impulse to gather and just hang around where blood's been spilled.

Now that I can drive, I always avoid that stretch of Route 57 where my mother was found. For a good year, people made a shrine out of the spot—white crosses, flowers, notes next to the lone linden tree. Unbearable.

When I was in the car with my dad, I'd look away, but he'd slow down, always studying, searching. Like something would jump out of the barren landscape and tell him how his wife's lifeless body ended up on the side of the road one winter night.

My dad was the one who found her there when she didn't come home after the town council meeting. His squad car headlights picking up her cobalt blue parka in the frigid pre-dawn

darkness. *Clothing askew... indications of attempted assault...*
Cause of death: blunt trauma to the head.

Dad doesn't know I've read the police report, but I have. I
had to know.

As I get closer to the station, I hear the woman with the
skunk-stripe hair from Shear Bliss say, "It's terrorists for sure.
Trying to prove it's not even safe in the heartland."

"Oh, come on now," says Al Nordgren. "It's plain old murder. Just like seven years ago."

"There was another murder?" says Skunk Stripe. "*My gosh.*
Who was murdered?"

"My mother," I say, pushing my way through. This shuts
them up. They part for me like I'm contagious.

Al asks me how my dad's doing. I say he's still in the ICU,
not conscious yet. Murmurs of sympathy ripple through the
crowd. Everyone knows Roy Pierce. Maybe it's not so bad that
they're gathered, I realize. This is a community thing. A wake, of
sorts.

I smile a grim little smile of thanks and finally make it to the
door. As I go inside, I hear Skunk Stripe whisper: "Someone
murdered her mother?"

"Never found him," someone offers.

I shut the door and take a deep breath.

Our police station is only a *station* in the loosest sense. It's
really just an office: Lance's desk up front near the door, June's
desk in the back, my dad's separate office behind that. No counter, no bullet-proof glass like they have in the cities. Gray-blue
walls with light brown paneled wainscoting—more like an insur-
ance office than a police station. My dad wanted it to be low-key,
accessible. A little *too* accessible, as it turned out.

Lew Jaruzcelski, the town coroner, is inside taking pictures.
Lew is sixty-something but looks older—the job has aged him, I
think. But he's focused and professional and it's comforting to
see him. Technically, he doesn't need to be here; the coroner

leaves with the body. But Lew knows there are no *actual* detectives on this case, so he's back and I'm grateful.

Lance is kneeling near him, fumbling with something. Still a wreck.

Lew looks up at me and frowns. "Margo? You shouldn't be here, honey."

I'm ready with a bluff: "It's okay. My dad told me to come down. He deputized me."

At this, Lew's face brightens. "He's awake? That's great news."

"Mm-hmm," I mumble, feeling like crap for lying. Made even worse by the ecstatic look on Lance's face. He stands up.

"*Thank God.* Can I talk to him? Oh heck, I'll just go over."

"No-o," I stutter. "He needs to rest."

Lance stands there uncertainly. I realize he's holding a fingerprinting kit. He's been trying to dust without gloves on, spilling powder everywhere. I take the kit away from him. "That's not how you do it, Lance."

"I… just wanted to help," he mumbles.

God almighty. This guy is a police deputy. Now I see why Dad won't let him carry a gun. He tried to train him, shooting tin cans in our backyard, but it was hopeless. My mom used to fuss over him because his parents were dead. Lay out the lasagna and blueberry crumble for him on Sunday evenings at our house. They felt sorry for him. But really, couldn't they have hooked him up with, say, a *stockboy* job? Something a little less… *important?*

"Go do crowd control," I tell him. "There should be yellow tape outside."

He nods, shaken enough to accept my authority.

"And after that go look for witnesses," I add.

He looks at me blankly.

"Just go up and down the street and ask questions," I tell him. "See if anyone saw anything, knows anything."

He's still hesitant.

"You can do it." I nudge him.

He gets his jacket, finds some yellow tape, and leaves.

Note to self: ask Dad why June insisted on hiring him. I mean, really. Then I clench up, remembering: *if* I can ask Dad. I turn around to find Lew appraising me. Trying to decide how much of my act he's buying. I turn it up a notch. "I'll try to stay out of your way, but my dad told me to bag and tag anything unusual I see."

"Uh-huh," he responds coolly. "You know how to do that?"

"Absolutely," I lie. How hard can it be? *You just need big eyes*, my dad would say. That's his term for being observant, noticing everything: *big eyes*.

I put gloves on and move closer to June's desk. The blood stains are still there: on the desk, on the floor. Dry and brownish now, not red like last night. The thought of *last night* sends a shock wave through my body. Looking out through the ambulance window as June's body was carried out in a long black bag.

I take a breath and repeat: *big eyes*. What's the same and what's different?

I cross to June's desk, a simple, black metal Staples number. I take inventory: a form file with printouts on fire safety, senior safety, carjacking facts, the domestic violence hotline. Vacant home check request forms. Firearms application forms. Her computer. And one yellow Post-it with a note in June's handwriting: "Talk to Mac."

Mac. I don't know anyone in town named Mac. Wait—did June have a MacBook, and she needed customer service? Doesn't seem very June-like. And wouldn't you say, "call Apple"? But June might not know that. Anyway, it's a clue. I carefully remove it and put it in an evidence bag.

Back to the search. I realize I need to get into her computer to check, among other things, who in town has firearms. But I don't know her password. It looks so easy on TV: *just check the computer*. I'll come back later and work on that with Hank.

As I consider this, something catches my eye: a smear of blood on the monitor. Two little swipes, June reached out and grazed it with her fingertips. Why? It doesn't take long for alarm bells to go off. *Because there's something in there she wants us to see*. She didn't have the strength to write a note so she smeared the computer with her blood, saying *look here*. I would try to check it now if Lew wasn't here. I *must* get into it later, I vow to myself. I take a picture with my cell, then move on.

Back to the desk: Cornhusker's pen cup. Bible-verse-of-the-day tear-off calendar. September 6th, Ephesians 6:16: *Above all, taking the shield of faith wherewith ye shall be able to quench all the fiery darts of the wicked.*

I stare at the quote. *The fiery darts of the wicked.* You're kidding me.

Is that a bag and tag? No, I decide. Just really weird.

Above the desk on the wall is a poster of the FBI's Ten Most Wanted Fugitives. All men: young, old, white, Latino. Wanted for murder, kidnapping, armed robbery, drug trafficking. I look at the faces: some acting tough, some scared, one or two with the blank visage of sociopaths. I'm sure June had them memorized. Could it have been one of these guys, drifting in from Route 80? Possibly. But not likely.

That was the popular theory with my mom: *assaulted by a drifter*. But really, I think no one wanted to believe it was someone she knew. Someone who's still here in Lazarus.

Motive and opportunity: these are the two homicide buzzwords that bounce around my head now. Motive: don't know yet. But opportunity? I ask Lew if he can tell the time of death yet. Last night, he says bluntly. Exact time TBD. I ask if he found shell casings: no. Does he have a make on the ammo yet? I can tell by the look on his face Lew's ready to pull the plug on Sherlock Junior here. *Not yet*, he allows, turning his back on me.

I glance over at the printer on a counter on the left. There's a piece of paper in the printout area. I cross and carefully lift it out. It appears to be a note June typed, which reads:

remind Roy:
- *prep for special council meeting on Sam Claypool's development Friday night*

Friday night. That's tonight.

key points to support rejection of plan:
- *location is zoned for at least five acres of land that is zoned agriculture. Sam must apply for variance (Ha! Good luck!)*
- *study (mine) shows that the starter homes Sam's proposing won't help attract a major shopping center like Papillon's Shadow Lake. Homes are too small and not worth enough money. (and knowing Sam, they'll be made on the cheap)*

general theme of objection: we're not stopping progress, we just believe Lazarus can do better!

Huh. This is not news exactly; Dad and June were always grumbling about Sam Claypool buying out poor, gullible farmers in order to build his "shanty town." But would Sam *kill* her for objecting to it? Also, Sam was at Back-to-School Night, a solid alibi. But maybe that's why he caused a scene with Dad, so people would remember he was there, while one of his henchmen… It seems too movie-ish, too dramatic. But then, June's dead. And there's definitely a motive here; she wanted his project *scrapped.* Another bag-and-tag.

I open June's drawers. The first thing I see chokes me up: a box of Girl Scout Thin Mints. *That's right, June loved her Thin Mints.* I used to sell them to her when I was a scout.

Keep looking: paper clips, Post-it pads, thumbtacks. Packets of Splenda. A key ring.

I see her purse under the desk. A sensible brown handbag. I pick it up.

Inside, there's a wallet: credit card, Shoprite, library card, no photos. One lipstick: Mahogany Red. Comb. Honda key. House key. No cell phone. June didn't have one. Her whole life was in this office and her house, both of which had phones. What did she need a cell phone for?

I look over at Lew, who's engrossed in his work, then pocket the house key.

What else? I sit in her chair and take the scene in. Nothing unusual, nothing out of place. Through the front windows, the familiar view of Marcy's faux stonework exterior.

But there's an itch in my chest. Something's not right.

I close my eyes and picture June at work. Brown cardigan draped over her chair in the fall, dark green in the winter. Blue light from her computer monitor reflecting off her glasses. On the phone. Jotting down notes in her...

That's it! June's big black logbook/diary is missing! She *always, always* had it, and guarded it like Pharaoh's treasure. I snooped in it once when I was younger and she snatched it up and smacked me with it. That's how important it was to her.

I call over to Lew: "Dr. Jaruzcelski—did you take anything out of the office?"

Something in my voice prompts a serious reply from the coroner.

"No ma'am," he says. "I never touch the crime scene."

He peers at me curiously over his glasses. My heart is racing.

SIXTEEN

HANK

To say time passes slowly in purgatory is a serious understatement. I've been standing here watching June wash her blouse for… hours? Or just minutes? It's hard to say.

I figure I'll give it one more try. "*Emmie James. She's my mother. I just need to know if she's the one who came into the station last night.*"

More stain rubbing. It's awkward in so many ways, not the least of which is that she's half dressed. Above her head, Cleopatra gazes inscrutably down.

Finally, something registers. She turns to me. "James? You're Hank James?"

"Yes. I'm Hank James."

"The boy who…"

"The boy who got killed on the highway this summer; yeah, that's me."

She frowns. "Terrible story. I know his family," she says.

"My family, yes, that's what I'm trying to…"

A new look comes into her eyes. Fear. "So you're... dead?" she asks.

"Yes," I answer softly. "And so are you."

She looks around the room, her hands starting to shake. "But...what is this place?" she begs me. Then, desperate: "Aren't I going? Am I not going to..."

She claps her hand to her mouth, stricken. I rush to reassure her. I know she's religious.

"I'm sure you're going. This," I say, waving an arm around. "This isn't permanent, it's just a way station. But before you go, I need to find out..."

She closes her eyes, mortified. Murmurs, "He doesn't forgive me."

"What? *Who?* Who doesn't forgive you?"

"For what I did. He *can't,*" she says. Sobbing, knees buckling. I cross to her, touch her shoulder. I can feel it but not in a solid way. Kind of like a shifting mass with an electric current running through it.

"I'm sure he forgives you," I offer. "What could you have done that was so bad?"

She wipes her eyes, still crying. "It was a long time ago. I tried to live a good life... *after*. I tried to make it right. But it wasn't enough."

I know I should just comfort her, have some ghost-to-ghost empathy, but I *have* to get the story. I feel like one of those soulless newspeople who shove microphones in the grieving family's faces. But here I go.

"June, were you involved in something, something someone wanted to punish you for?"

She looks up at me, childlike now, eyes wide. Whispers, "I'm being punished?"

"No, I mean whoever shot you. Were they trying to keep you quiet about something?"

Her eyes narrow, and I see adult June return. She fixes her glasses, trying to remember. "I was waiting for him. I wanted to talk to him."

Relief floods my body. "*He*. So it was a he," I say.

She hesitates, suddenly unsure. "I felt so bad for her. For both of them."

Oh crap. "But it was a *man* you were waiting for. You said *he*," I remind her.

She's lost again.

"June, what else do you remember about the person who came in?"

I realize I'm shaking her shoulder—which is wobbling under my hand—and stop. After a long, purgatory-time pause, she finally replies: "Chesapeake."

I stare at her. "Chesapeake," I repeat.

"Yes. Chesapeake. It surprised me."

My wheels are turning so fast now they're grinding. *Chesapeake*, it's a bay back East, somewhere near DC, Maryland, crab cakes, what the hell...?

"What does that mean? This guy was from... the Chesapeake area?"

My interrogation is interrupted by the sound of music. *Oh no*—I know what it is. I'm out of time.

"Is it a name? A code?" I plead. "What does Chesapeake mean, June?"

But she's not listening to me anymore. She's stopped crying and light is coming back into her eyes.

"June, *please!*"

The music's getting louder. She follows it out the door.

We're in the lobby now and the light show has begun. The pharaoh mural at the top of the stairs is glowing. The colors are so vivid—the blue Nile, golden pyramids—it looks almost real, like a gateway to an ancient realm. And the music is, well, *heavenly*. Chimes, beautiful deep tones, choral harmonies. A sound like home, laughter, and salvation all rolled into one. It's intoxicating.

June's face is radiant now as she moves towards the stairs. So happy, she almost glides.

"June?" I try just one more time. "Before you go, can't you please tell me who killed you?"

She turns to me, and for a moment, I think I might get my answer. But she just smiles and says, "It doesn't matter." Then, looking back at the mural: "I'm grateful."

And with that, she starts up the stairs. Slowly, starting to glow herself as she gets closer to the top.

As I watch her, my heart starts to swell with... what? Longing? *Yes.* In this moment, I'd like to follow her up those stairs. Leave this whole mess behind. Why not?

I actually have to steady myself, *root* myself to the floor to keep from doing it. I hear myself repeating, "Margo, Margo, Margo..."

And then, with a sudden flood of light and a loud *WHOOSH*, June's body is swept upwards. A mind-blowing mini-Rapture, a thunderous ascension, then nothing. June is gone.

And all is back to normal in the theater. No lights, no angelic music. Just me, alone again. With a wrenching pain in my chest that feels like heartbreak.

SEVENTEEN

MARGO

Chesapeake Energy Corporation, the second largest producer of natural gas. Chesapeake, Virginia. Chesapeake Bay, an estuary lying inland from the Atlantic Ocean. *Chesapeake*, an epic novel by James A. Michener. Chesapeake Bay Beach Club. Chesapeake puppies. Chesapeake Community College.

Hank and I have been Google searching "Chesapeake" for half an hour now and that's what we've got. It's all back-East-type stuff that I can't for the life of me connect with June. My brain is on Chesapeake overload: puppies swimming with James Michener in an estuary near a college. Hank can't make sense of it either.

As for "Mac," neither of us can think of anyone with that name or nickname. I'll have to ask Dad.

We're still at the police station, working on Dad's computer. *That* password I know: Margo9. He used to let me hang out after school here and play on the computer after my mom died; hence the "9." That's how old I was.

It's weird being in here without him. His wonderfully Dad-sloppy desk. Folders upon folders: on the desk, on shelves, on the floor. A poster of Clint Eastwood in some Western. Dad's a big Clint fan.

I don't like the feeling that I'm replacing him in here, that I'm trying to wear a hat that's too big for me. But there's a job to be done, right, June?

One good thing from Hank's report: at least his mom is off the hook. Hank says June definitely said it was a man who shot her. Someone she knew. But *who?*

"You're *sure* that's all she said?" I bug him again.

"Yes. Just 'Chesapeake. It surprised me.' Then the music started and I lost her."

A look has come over Hank's face. Something I can't place.

"What was it like?" I ask him. "The music."

"*Incredible,*" he murmurs, and I realize the look is *longing.* Longing to go up those stairs.

I get a sick feeling in my gut. *I'm* the one holding him back, keeping him in limbo. It's not fair.

But I *need* Hank, plain and simple. His laughing, uplifting blue eyes, behind glasses. Innocent in a way, his life untouched by tragedy... What am I saying, he's *dead.* And I've kept him here, or a Higher Power has kept him here for me, or he's *insist-ed* on staying and *Oh thank God* because I still need to bathe in those two blue pools of light. It's a grace, really it is, Hank's lin-gering. But is it fair to him?

I take a breath, gather my courage. "Hank," I say gently. "You can go if you want. I don't want to keep you here."

"I *can't* go, Marg," he responds. "I think... I'm supposed to help you with something."

I nod. Okay...

"What is it you *want?*" he asks me point blank.

"You alive," I answer. "Mom alive, June at her desk, keep-ing tabs on the town..."

"That's all a given," Hank says softly. "But I can't make it happen. I *can* help you investigate June's murder; we're in that together. But... something else. What do you really want, down deep?"

I know the answer immediately; it's not down that deep.

"I want to sleep soundly again," I blurt.

Hank nods, getting it. *Yeah.*

Now it shoots out of me like a firehose. "After my mom died, my dreams were full of murderers. Since you died, I hear screeching tires, see you flying up in the air, hear your body smack down on the pavement. And now with June, I barely sleep at all. Maybe all this sleeplessness has sent me over the edge. Maybe that's why I see you."

Hank nods again, indulging this possibility.

"Okay," he murmurs. "You want to sleep well."

"No!" I counter, dizzied by my own one-eighty. "Not really. Because I'm afraid I'll *miss* something. I must have missed a lot of things: clues, hints, *signs* that could have kept everyone I love from dying."

I'm crying now, and Hank does our new thing, where he circles me with his arms. An air hug.

"We'll start with June, honey," he whispers. "We'll get all this solved so you can sleep again."

I'm sobbing now and I swear I can feel his arms around me. Holding me up. That's how strong our love is.

The door flies open. It's Lance, hair askew, face sweaty from doing actual police work. I wipe away my tears, shift back into faux deputy mode.

"Hey. What did you find out?"

"Did you know she colored her hair?" he offers. "I didn't."

I sigh. "That's great. Anything else?"

"Well, Buddy at Shell said she got new tires on her Subaru last spring. She was real pleased with 'em."

I nod. Awesome.

"She liked birds," he continues. "Did you know that? She'd go into the pet shop and look at the parakeets."

Hank puts his feet up on the desk, noting, "Maybe the birds didn't like that. All that staring. Maybe one of 'em had a grudge against her."

I ignore this, ask Lance what else he's got. He has to think for a minute, then reveals:

"Mimi at the haircutters said something weird. She said she always thought June liked women. You know, in *that* way. And then Dawn Fletcher said no, she was pretty sure she'd had something going with that crazy old guy, the radio preacher? She'd seen them at church together years ago and thought there was something going on."

Hank takes his feet down.

"Gib Hawkins," he says. "He's Ted Hawkins' father."

I get my jacket then tell Lance, "I think we'd better pay Mr. Hawkins a visit."

Lance looks at me, unsure. "Don't you think we should wait and let your dad handle this?"

I shoot him my toughest look. "The first forty-eight hours, Lance. That's the crucial time for solving a crime."

It sounds so TV, but it's true. Lance is still hesitant.

"Besides," I add. "We don't know if my dad is going to wake up."

Lance looks at me. "I thought you said he's awake," he says. "He deputized you."

Right; forgot about that. I don't have the time or headspace right now to keep track of a fib. A *fib*, not a lie, because I *had* to get going on this. I tell Lance:

"He goes in and out. He's very weak."

I feel like crap for finessing Dad's health crisis to suit my immediate needs. But it works. Lance nods, sadly re-zips his jacket. As I push the door open, I notice my arm is shaking. Some tough cop I am.

EIGHTEEN

HANK

I wish I hadn't watched so many horror movies. Because pulling up to the Hawkins house—isolated Nebraska farmhouse, sky dark with rainclouds, front door hanging open—I am seriously creeped out. It's like a prairie Bates Motel, minus the neon sign.

I don't like Margo going in there by herself (let's face it, going in with Lance is going by herself) when I can't protect her. But I know the look on her face: there's no stopping her.

Then it occurs to me: I can go in first. I rode over with Margo and Lance, sitting in the back, once again forgetting I'm dead.

When I tell her to wait, she looks over at Lance.

"I don't think he's in any hurry to go in, Marg."

Indeed, Lance is hunched over like a scared little elf. Margo nods and I pop into Gib Hawkins' kitchen.

The first thing I notice is the music: some '80s song blaring from a cassette boombox. "Hit Me With Your Best Shot." Pat something, I think. The room: dirty white cabinets that go all the way to the ceiling, littered counters (half-eaten food as well as cruddy dishes), cracked, worn black linoleum floor tiles.

The other thing that does not escape my attention is that Gib—a spidery old cuss if there ever was one—is sitting at the kitchen table cleaning a shotgun. And he's drunk—Schlitz empties abound. Not a good combination.

He's slurring, fumbling along with the song: *"...your best shhot!"* Spittle sprays. Then an even louder: *"Fire 'wa-a-ay!"*

He loads the gun. Drops a bullet. Picks it up.

I do not like this one bit.

One more detail: on the far side of the kitchen there's a large black-and-white picture of a younger June Hudspeth. It's attached to the top of a dress form with a yellow dress on it.

All of which adds up to *yikes.*

I pop out to the car, but Margo and Lance aren't there.

I pop back into the kitchen just as Margo pushes the door open, saying, "Mr. Hawkins? Your door was open."

I yell at her to get the hell out but she's frozen, assessing the situation. Lance is behind her, trying to see over her shoulder.

Gib whirls around, points the shotgun at her. There's nothing I can do to stop a bullet if he shoots.

But Margo's amazingly levelheaded: she starts talking to him in the calmest cop voice imaginable, considering she has to yell over an '80s pop song.

"We didn't mean to disturb you. We're from the Lazarus police department. We just want to talk with you."

Gib looks at her blearily, confused. The barrel of the gun wavers.

Margo starts sidestepping, *very* slowly, over to the boombox. Turns it off.

"There," she says, like a kindergarten teacher. "That's better."

"Who the hell are you?" Gib snarls.

"Margo Pierce, sir; Chief Pierce's daughter. And this is Deputy Lance Ritter."

Lance is too scared to speak. He keeps looking at the gun. Then over to the dress form. Then back at the gun.

Gib grunts a response.

Margo keeps going: "This must be a hard time for you. I understand you knew the deceased."

Gib looks down, wincing. "Who gives a damn?" he mutters.

"Excuse me?" Margo asks brightly.

"Jesus, Margo, just get out," I tell her. She doesn't. She's on a mission.

Gib gazes foggily at the picture of June.

"Do you think I care about your pretty little legs anymore? Clip-clopping down the street in those tan sandals. Do you think I even *notice*?"

Lance whispers into Margo's ear, "Why is he talking about your legs?"

Margo shakes her head, shoots back, "He's not talking about *my* legs, Lance." Then, to Gib: "You could really help us out, Mr. Hawkins." She nods to the dress form. "You were obviously… close to Miss Hudspeth."

Gib frowns. Steadies his gun in his lap. Says, "I think you need to leave."

But Margo can't stop: "I can see you're grieving. But if there's any insight you can provide…"

Gib fixes Margo with a cold stare. "I didn't know her."

"Okay," I say. "He didn't know her. Let's go."

But Margo thinks she's a real detective and keeps going. "With all due respect, sir, you've got a large picture of the deceased right there."

"Get out," Gib growls.

Lance has had enough. "Okay!" he says. "I can see this is a bad time…"

He tries to pull Margo out but she's not budging. She keeps her soft, good-cop purr going: "She's dead, Mr. Hawkins. Someone murdered your friend. I'm sure you want to know who as much as we do."

I can't take it anymore and pop right next to Margo. "Do you think you're bulletproof? The guy has a gun!"

Margo keeps going. Maybe she thinks her hipster faux army surplus jacket makes her a soldier. "How long had you known her?"

I yell right in her face: *"This is not brave, Margo, it's just stupid! You don't try to question a drunk guy with a gun!"*

Gib is staring into space now. He says to no one: "You think you can leave me? You think it's gonna kill me?"

"We should really get going..." Lance whines.

"How about some coffee?" asks Margo.

"Coffee?" I scream. *"Really?"*

Gib lets out a loud bellow of pain, picks up the gun and shoots a hole in the dress form's chest. Then slumps backward.

The three of us just stare. Then Margo finally looks at me, wide-eyed. Not so tough anymore.

"Just walk out the door, sweetie," I tell her. "You don't want to die. Trust me."

Margo hesitates, then says, "I'm sorry we took up your time. We'll be going now."

Lance's legs barely work as he stumbles out ahead of her through the dark detritus in the front hall.

Back in the car, Lance and I are still tripped out, but Margo's oddly exhilarated. "He's a gun owner and he was obsessed with her. *He just shot her in the chest.*"

"He just shot a mannequin in the chest," I counter.

"A mannequin with her picture on it. He's definitely a suspect."

"I don't know," I say. "It's pretty clear he was in love with her. Why would he kill her?"

"I don't know," Margo replies, eyes blazing. "But I plan to find out."

She's too stoked to care that she's talking to me in front of Lance. But Lance is too freaked to care. She could be singing Coldplay in French, he wouldn't notice.

A pinging sound: Margo's getting a text.

She checks her phone. Her jaw drops.

"It's from my dad."

NINETEEN

MARGO

My dad's chalk-white face is the most beautiful thing I've ever seen. I want to throw my arms around his neck, lie next to him, and just sob. But Lance is with me, so I can't.

His hospital room is a Hallmark store of get-well cards and balloons. Seems like everyone in town has sent something.

"There's my girl," he whispers when he sees me. I take the seat next to his bed and hold his hand.

A flood of words fills my head: I was so worried, you're my life, my whole family, *please, please* get better.

But I just ask him how he's feeling. He tries to muster up a smile, drop his voice to a reassuring baritone, but it's a little creaky.

"Fantastic," he murmurs. "Doc says I can QB the Huskers tomorrow."

Now my tears come, through a crazy big smile of relief. He squeezes my hand. Lance shifts uncomfortably from foot to foot. Clears his throat.

Dad looks at him, shifts into Chief Roy mode. "I'm going to need your help, Lance. This is serious now. I need you to step up."

"Yes sir." Lance nods.

This exchange stirs something in me. Something like sibling rivalry. Why isn't he asking *me* to step up?

"Dad," I say. "I already checked the station for clues. June's diary is missing and there's a smear of blood on her monitor. I think she was trying to tell us..."

The color returns to Dad's face, but not in a good way. "Margo you are *not to investigate this case*. Do you understand me?"

I hesitate. *But you're sick, Lance is useless, and also do you know anyone named Mac?*

He drives the point home: "We're dealing with a *murder* here. You're sixteen years old. You are to go to school, help me at home, and that's it. Got it?"

There's no answer but yes. I nod. He turns back to Lance.

"I need you to take June's computer home and check the search history. Can you do that?"

Lance nods like a bobblehead. I can't believe Dad's entrusting this to him.

I want to tell Dad about Gib Hawkins, but the fact that the man pointed a shotgun at me might bring on another heart attack. I try another approach.

"Lance," I say. "Tell Dad what you told me about Gib Hawkins."

Lance looks at me, unsure. I prompt him: "You got a tip and followed it up? Went over to his house?"

Lance gets it and tells the Gib story, minus me. I force myself not to correct him on some of the details. At least Dad's got the idea: crazy gun-toting guy who's obsessed with June.

After Lance finishes the story, Dad just nods and asks him to give us a moment. Lance leaves.

Now Dad turns to me, the fire definitely back in his eyes.

"You took it upon yourself to question a suspect. To go to a strange man's house with no protection, no training."

I forgot: my dad misses nothing. Even weakened, even in a frayed seafoam green hospital gown, he's still the chief of police.

He continues: "I should lock you in the goddamned house."

"But Dad," I argue. "This is *June!* I want to do *something!*"

He stares at me for a minute, weighing his reply. "Okay," he says. "You can drive me to the town council meeting tonight."

Now it's my turn to be tough. *"No way,"* I tell him. "You just had a heart attack. What're you gonna do, drag your machines and monitors with you?"

"Fine," he says. "I'll drive myself."

I know how stubborn he is, so I just say I'll pick him up at 6:30.

Out in the hallway, I catch up with Lance (more shimmering golden tile on the walls; I hate it). When I tell him not to worry, I'll check June's computer, he turns to me, red in the face.

"I know how to scan a computer!" he yells. "I'm not an idiot. *I'm* the deputy!"

He practically spits the words at me. I've never seen him like this before. I try to backpedal: "Of course you are, I didn't mean to suggest…"

He cuts me off: "He wants *my* help, not yours. I'm the one who gets to save people now!"

And with that, he's off down the hall. As I watch him go, an old movie title comes to me: *The Mouse that Roared.*

HANK

The truth is, I agree with Roy. I don't really want Margo to investigate June's murder, particularly after the Zonked Old Gun Guy incident. I want her to finish high school, go to college, do something cool and artsy, and crap, even get married and have kids, I guess. Not loving that last part, but I want her to have a *life*, and that shotgun shook me up.

I was there in the hospital room, with her and Roy and Lance. I don't always materialize when I know Margo doesn't want to be distracted, but I think she knew I was there.

So now I'm torn between agreeing with Roy and helping Margo solve June's murder. The best thing I can do, I decide, is do as much gumshoe work on my own as I can, Casper-style.

As I pop back to Gib's place, I actually feel a sense of purpose for the first time since I died. I didn't get to accomplish much in life, but maybe I can do something useful with my death.

I'm in Gib's living room, the decor of which I can only describe as "isolated farmhouse gothic." An old, beat-to-hell wing chair. A moss green velvet-upholstered settee from a couple of centuries ago. Yellowed lace curtains. Women's magazines from the '80s on a coffee table. A framed picture of a collie on one wall. An ancient lamp with actual cobwebs hanging off it. The only thing missing, creepy-old-house wise, is a skeleton in a wedding gown propped up in a rocking chair.

I can hear Gib moving around in the basement, but I decide to do my snooping up here. Even though I know he can't shoot me, I'd rather not be in the same room with him. It's comical, I realize—the living giving the dead the willies. Such are the ironies of my new state.

I move into the dining room. Faded wallpaper; cherry print on a white background. The dining table is covered with random stuff: punchbowl, coffee pot, box of shotgun pellets, bottle of hydrogen peroxide, cowgirl doll.

Contrasting with this chaos is a corner china cabinet. Nice old dishes and a tea service sit protected from the dishevellitude behind dusty glass. Which, along with the magazines, tells me that at some point a normal woman lived here.

On the wall, there's a framed map of Nebraska territory in the 1800s. In another corner, a grandfather clock stopped at 7:30. Which is perfect, because the whole place feels like life just stopped here at some point.

One interesting detail: on a sideboard against the wall are several framed pictures, all turned face down. I wish I could pick them up, but I can't.

I move down the hall and into an open room. It's a sick room: there's a stripped hospital bed, a bed pan, an IV stand. A book on a nightstand: *To Kill A Mockingbird*. And here, finally, a framed picture I can see. It's of a boy, around eleven or twelve. Ted.

A memory comes back to me: Mom snapping at me and Boyd for making faces behind Gib's back downtown years ago.

He was looking particularly demented and, well, it seemed to call for comedy.

"You don't know what that man's been through," Mom hissed at us, once she'd hustled us into the car. "I saw it: his poor wife almost bald from the cancer treatments. The house a mess, that boy half-starved. I brought dinners over; everyone did. Just *awful*."

Boyd and I looked down at our flip-flops, guilty. That *would* totally suck. It *did*; I can feel it in this room.

I hear a sound nearby and jump. Someone's on this floor. I can see a closed door across the hall. The noise is coming from inside that room. I remind myself that no one can hurt me, and pop over.

I'm in Ted's room. I know this because Ted is sitting on a chair in front of me. *Holy crap*, I realize, *the guy lives here.* No wonder he's having an affair, he just wants to get out of the old man's house.

The contrast with the rest of the house is startling; I feel like I'm in a Pottery Barn store. Everything's modern and tasteful: all white, brown, and beige. Even the pictures on the wall are neutral, impersonal, like they were ordered from a catalogue. There's a bookshelf full of literary classics, a neat desk stacked with his classwork.

The resounding question here is why is this guy living at home with Daddy Nutcase? He's got a good job, he could get his own place.

I notice a framed diploma over his desk: University of Chicago. Good school. Which leads to another question: Why would a UC graduate come back to Lazarus? Mom's gone, Dad's wacked. He's a good-looking guy, he could be living it up in a city somewhere, not sneaking around some backwater with a married woman.

At the moment, he looks spent, worn-down, like he hasn't slept. But is it guilty murderer insomnia or what-the-hell-am-I-doing-in-this-crazy-ass-town exhaustion?

I hear music from downstairs. Something churchy—a hymn, I think. Ted gets up, goes to the closet, and finds a shirt. I pop downstairs.

First and foremost, there's no missing the giant wooden cross in Gib's basement. Eight feet tall, roughhewn 6" x 6"s fitted and nailed together. It's a real Jesus cross, one you could crucify someone on. *Okaaay*.

On the other side of the room is a transmitter, a switchboard, and Gib himself, seated in a chair in front of a microphone.

I'm in Gib's radio station.

Gib turns the music down and speaks into the mic.

"Brethren, today is a dark day. I will not read from scripture today as I must attend to another matter. A good woman, a sister in Christ, was taken to live with the angels last night. And she did not die a peaceful death; no, she was struck down by the worst kind of sinner."

Suddenly, the thunder of footsteps on the stairs. Gib keeps talking.

"I do not believe it is against God's plan to seek justice for June Hudspeth. He has given us free will, as you know, and when man uses this will with contempt for His laws..."

Ted appears, angry now.

"The most *central* law of the tablets, thou shall not kill—"

Ted crosses the room and grabs the mic. Gib lunges for him; the two wrestle, ending up on the floor. Ted, the stronger of the two, prevails. He pushes his father off him, stands, and yanks the mic cord out of the console.

Gib glares up at him, panting. Then growls: "Why do you seek to silence me? What are you hiding?"

Ted's eyes are blazing. I'm starting to see the family resemblance.

"Dad, do you really want the police snooping around here?"

"Already have been. Some deputy was here with a girl. The chief's daughter."

Ted blinks. It takes him a minute to respond. Finally he says: "Margo Pierce. Margo Pierce was here?"

For some reason I don't like the way he says her name. I don't like him knowing this.

Gib just grunts.

"What did she want?" Ted asks.

"She knows," says Gib.

At this Ted kneels down and shakes his father. "She knows *what*, Dad? What does she know?"

"*That I loved her!*" Gib shouts, crumbling into tears. Ted lets him go, stands back up. Stares and thinks. Then heads for the stairs.

Gib calls after him: *"What are you trying to hide? Your shame? The shame she concealed for you?"*

But Ted's gone.

The old man curls on to his knees and sobs. His hunched-over shape reminds me of an armadillo: protecting itself but still tough.

TWENTY-ONE

MARGO

The town council meeting is packed. You can feel the anxiety, the need to gather on this night after the murder. After all, there's a killer on the loose.

Sometimes people dress up for these events, but in light of current events, no one cares. The men are mostly in jeans and plaid, a couple of farmers wear gimme caps. Women in fall color sweaters, arms crossed, guarding themselves. One of their own was just *shot*, for God's sake.

I myself—always an avatar of symbolic clothing—am wearing a power-red jacket, quasi-military style. It felt right when I put it on, but now, given the fearful vibe in the room, it feels over the top. These people need reassurance, not Michael Jackson escorting their ailing protector.

Dad and I are late. They didn't try to stop him at the hospital (no one tells Chief Roy no) but they did insist he leave in a wheelchair. So with all the maneuvering, packing it into the car, setting it up again, we're fifteen minutes late.

Dad wants to walk in but just getting out of the car tires him. He finally agrees to be wheeled in. Inside, it's standing room only. People are lined up against the walls. Even some kids I know from school are here, like Hank's friends Ty and Jase. We nod awkwardly at each other across the room. I used to hang with them all the time, but there's space between us since Hank died. Just too painful, I guess.

Another reason it's trippy to be in this room is that this was the last place my mom was seen the night she died. She was dedicated to the town council. I used to come with her to meetings if Dad was working late. I'd just sit with a coloring book or whatever. But I was fascinated with a mural that still spans the wall opposite the door: noble Indians and buckskinned settlers meeting on the windswept plains of Nebraska. The whole thing, including the landscape, is just so epic, so not like anything I've ever seen from a car window in my home state. I get a surge of nostalgia, seeing it again and remembering that curious, innocent child there with her mom. *Me.*

I look down at my red jacket—another thrift store triumph—and suddenly it makes me feel lonely. I always notice girls out clothes shopping with their mothers. Maybe that's why I'm so into clothes: I'm compensating. There's no one to take me to the mall, to show outfits to, so I'm determined to have more *style* than anyone in this Podunk town. I check out fashion-forward websites, find special pieces in vintage stores; for some reason, I want clothes with *meaning.* I'm on my own in this—Dad doesn't care about fashion—so I'm determined to be *unique.*

If Mom was still here, I'd probably be an ordinary American-Eagle-jeans-and-logo-tees girl. And that would be fine. Better than fine, that would be great. To be ordinary, to not always be leaning into a cold wind. But I'm not ordinary; tonight I'm a scarlet soldier heading into battle.

As I wheel Dad in, a collective gasp goes up. Then cheers, even some applause. Dad nods, embarrassed.

The head councilman, Dan Svenson, has started the meeting, but has to stop while everyone gathers around Roy Pierce. They ask how he feels, cry, reach out to touch him like he's the risen Messiah. The survivor. Sweet old Mrs. McNamara, my Sunday School teacher, takes his hand and holds it for a moment, tears in her eyes. Mrs. McNamara. As I look around the room, I also notice the McLeans and the MacAllisters. All "Macs," I realize, like Sully's a nickname for Sullivan. The McLeans have two kids in school; Darcy McLean is a year younger than me. No idea where they work. And the MacAllisters are retirees with grown kids. But did June know any of them? Looking around at the five Macs, I can't put it together. Why would she want to talk to them? I make a mental note to have Hank snoop.

The group hug is interrupted by Dr. James, who wades through and plants himself in front of Dad. He is not happy.

"Are you *kidding*, Roy? What the hell do you think you're doing?"

My dad replies calmly that he's here for the meeting.

"*No,*" Dr. James counters. "Uh-uh. Margo, get him back to the hospital."

I shrug helplessly, feeling ridiculous. Of course he's right.

Irritated, Dr. James brushes me out of the way to wheel Dad himself.

Suddenly, a shout from someone in the crowd: "Who did it, Roy?"

A hush falls over the assembly. Before Dad can respond, someone else speaks up.

"He doesn't know. He never figured out who killed his own wife, you think he'll solve this one?"

It's Sam Claypool, standing in the front of the room. Tonight he's wearing a blue suit with a garnet tie; the guy always looks like he's running for office.

The crowd's reaction is swift and harsh. Anger, condemnation, a shove to Sam's shoulder. But Sam just keeps staring at my dad, his eyes sparkling with that predatory look of his.

And suddenly it hits me, clear as a bell: *Sam Claypool wants to kill my dad.* I think he's actually trying to bring on another heart attack. He wants Dad gone so he can take over the town. This isn't a lame high school rivalry anymore; this is serious. And if he's willing to shoot my dad through the heart with a comment like that, what else might he have been willing to do?

Dad's trying to speak, but he can't be heard over the din. It doesn't help that he doesn't have full command of his voice. Sam's trying to say something else, but he can't be heard either, so he crosses to the mic at the podium.

He stares the group down, then: "Say what you want about me, but you know I'm just saying what a lot of you have been thinking today."

This quiets the room down, which is crushing. Because it means he's right.

He continues: "The last murder in this town has gone unsolved for *seven years.* Now we've got another on our hands. I know everybody loves Chief Roy, but do you really trust him to sort this out?"

There's some resistance to this, shouts of support for Dad, but Sam keeps going.

"I'm just saying, maybe it's time to get some help. Get some detectives over from Norfolk, FBI, whatever it takes for us to feel safe in our homes again."

God, he's a good politician. I can feel him starting to win them over. But does he really mean that, about calling the FBI in? A guilty man wouldn't do it. Or is it just another con?

Sam goes on, in a silkier tone: "Look, I have a lot invested in this town. As many of you know, I'm building a new development, and I'm making headway on attracting a corporate headquarters to Lazarus. All that growth is going to revitalize the local economy, create jobs, and raise your property values. But if Lazarus becomes the unsolved murder capital of the Great Plains, who's gonna want to move here?"

Some murmurs of assent now. Team Roy is slowly being won over to Team Sam.

Dad's gesturing to me; I lean down.

"Get me the mic," he whispers.

Sam's still speechifying as I head up to the podium. He looks at me, startled, as I unhook the mic from its holder. Before he can stop me, I say into the mic: "Chief Roy wants to say something." Then bring it back to him.

Total silence now, as Dad takes the mic with a shaky hand.

I hate this, I think. I hate that Dad's in a wheelchair and Sam's at the podium winning hearts and minds. *Come on, Dad.*

He starts to speak, softly but clearly.

"Sam's got a point," he says.

My heart sinks.

"My wife's murder has hung over this town for seven years. No one knows that better than me. And now, with what happened last night, you've got a right to be concerned."

He pauses. For a minute it seems like he might just stop there, but he's just gathering strength. Finally: "I know I'm not in the best shape, but I *swear* to you, my deputy and I are on this."

A loud snicker from the podium.

"Where's your deputy tonight? Home cleaning his slingshot?"

Dad fires right back at him, the only time he raises his voice: "Actually, he's out working the case." He takes a breath, then finishes up. "I'll make a deal with you," he says to the townspeople. "If I don't have the killer in custody by Thanksgiving, you can replace me. Okay?"

Confusion now. Shouts of loyalty to Dad mixed with "sounds right to me" murmurs.

Dad doesn't wait for it to all shake out. He pulls on my sleeve, whispers, "Take me back."

As I wheel him up the aisle—the whole town arguing, calling out to us—all I can think is, *I have to get this case solved by Thanksgiving.*

TWENTY-TWO

HANK

'Ve followed Ted over to the Claypools' house. A stately white power-trip manor with white columns out front—the showiest house in town. As Carolyn lets him in the back door, I realize something. Of course, Sam's at the town council meeting. Perfect time for a hook-up.

So now I'm spying on them in the basement rec room as Ted paces and Carolyn drinks.

The room is all Sam Claypool: pool table, bowling trophies, a huge mounted bass on the wall. All it needs, machismo-wise, is Papa Hemingway drinking a whiskey at the bar. Carolyn probably enjoys bringing her lover into Sam's man cave. It's the icing on the forbidden love cake.

I didn't like the look on Ted's face when his father told him Margo had been over. First shock, then anger. Why would a visit from the police—not even the real police, just Margo and Lance—be a threat unless he was guilty of something?

And what's "the shame that she concealed for you"? Did June cover up something for Ted and then decide to expose him? I need to get the whole story.

The irony here is that the person who taught me how to get the whole story was Ted Hawkins. He's the one who drilled all the journalistic "who, what, when, where, why" into me.

The sad and confusing thing now is that I really felt a bond with him. He was always the smartest guy in the room, the wittiest. I looked up to him, tried to keep up with him. And here he is now looking guilty of *something*, pacing in his mistress's basement.

He's talking about Margo now.

"Why in the hell would they come over to our place? What do they know?"

"They're probably just talking to everyone who knew her," says Carolyn, stretched out on the leather couch like a lazy cat.

"But how did they find out about June and Dad? They were *very, very* discreet—never even spoke in town. After all, my mom was still alive when it started."

Okay. Interesting.

"You're overthinking it," purrs Carolyn. "C'mon, have a drink."

She gets up, crosses to the bar, and pours him one. The woman is remarkably calm if she's an accessory to a murder. She brings him the drink; he doesn't take it. She puts it on the pool table.

"I just... I just need to know what they *know*," Ted whimpers, sounding younger and younger.

Carolyn perches on the edge of the pool table and pulls him to her. "I don't want this to get in the way of *our* plans," she says, stroking his hair. She's got him between her legs now. It's pretty clear what persuasive tools she's planning to use.

But Ted's not biting; he pulls away. "Seriously? You want to talk about *that* now? With everything going on?"

She grabs him by the shirt, not f-ing around anymore. "I'm talking about *freedom*," she says. "Getting out of here, leaving all this behind."

He looks into her eyes, considering. Then breaks away, sits on the couch. "It's not that simple."

"Sure it is," asserts Carolyn.

"You're living in a dreamworld. Where we, what, run away and play on the beach in Thailand for the rest of our lives? It *won't work*."

Okay, it's a run-off-together plan. Maybe Sam's not dead meat after all. Unless Carolyn wants her widow's pension before she goes.

"It's worth a try," sulks Carolyn, drinking Ted's drink.

Ted stares at her. Then finally, firmly: "This has gone too far. This whole thing has gone too far."

Carolyn closes her legs, sits up. "You mean... everything? *Us?*"

Ted takes a breath. Nods.

Now the cat is pissed off. If she could arch her back and hiss, she would. Her eyes turn vengeful.

"How do you think the people of this town would react if they knew you were in the car with me that night? The night that kid died?"

I know that kid. That kid is me.

The lovers stare each other down.

Then, suddenly, almost in slow motion, an oar leaning against the wall across the room falls to the floor.

Just behind it, through an open door, I see movement. Someone retreating into darkness. I'm not the only spy here.

Ted and Carolyn jump, stare at the oar. Then Ted slowly moves towards the open door.

I pop into the little room. It's a laundry room. I take a quick look around—no one here.

But there's another door, open to an unfinished part of the basement. I head in there and look around, but it's dark. Interesting side note: ghosts don't see better than anyone else in the dark.

Ted enters the laundry room behind me, turns on the light. Now I can see skis, storage boxes, a water heater, a furnace…and just behind the furnace, the very tip of a brown boot. I know these boots. They're my mother's.

I pop closer and there she is, crouching behind the furnace. *Oh Mom. No.*

Ted comes in, pulls a string light on. Mom slowly pulls her foot backward into darkness. Holds her breath.

Ted peers around, a fierce look on his face. The look of a killer?

I wish I could move something, make a branch fall outside. Anything to distract him. *Maybe if I concentrate…* but no. I'm powerless.

Ted squints. Moves towards the furnace. I feel my mother tense up.

He's four feet away when he stumbles, almost falls. Because there's a cat between his legs. A real cat.

Ted recovers his balance, picks the cat up.

"Hey Tiger. Was that you?"

He turns the light off, takes the cat back into the rec room. I hear my mother breathe. *Thank you, Tiger.*

It's not long before Ted leaves. I don't hear the rest of the conversation; I stay in the back with my mom. This is the apotheosis of my worries about her: crouching in a stranger's boiler room, hair and eyes wild. She looks like a crazed, naughty elf.

She waits a good ten minutes after Carolyn goes upstairs, then lets herself out the back door. Runs to her car a couple of blocks away, then drives home.

When my dad gets home from the town council meeting, Mom tells him the whole story, pacing again. Says she knows

Carolyn's secret. Dad hangs his head as he listens, and for a minute I think he's just going to gently guide her up to bed. But then I see his hands are tensed into fists. And when he finally lifts his head to look at her, there's a sparkle of rage in his eyes.

"You *broke into their house?*" he growls down at her.

"I needed to know..." Mom falters.

Dad's mouth is a hard, straight line. "Do you know what all my patients have been asking me?" It's a rhetorical question; Mom just blinks.

"How's Emmie?" he says evenly. "And not the usual 'how's Emmie?' in sympathy about Hank. This is about Back-to-School Night. Something between you and Carolyn Claypool. What happened, Emmie?"

That's right, it occurs to me. Dad wasn't there that night.

Mom looks down. "Nothing," she murmurs. "I... left."

"I found the gun," Dad says. "In your purse." Then tougher: *"What were you planning to do?!"*

At this, my mom just waves an arm helplessly and sits down on the couch. Dad sighs.

"Go to bed," he tells her. "And don't forget your pill."

There's no kindness in his voice. No understanding, which is not like him. After Mom climbs the stairs, Dad goes into his study. I follow him. He gets a key, opens the bottom drawer of his desk.

The gun is in there, plus a box of ammo. There's Cyrillic writing on the ammo box; it appears to be Russian. Dad holds the pistol in his hand for a minute, thinking something through. I hold my breath. Nothing is right with this picture.

He makes his decision, empties the ammo out of the pistol. Puts the gun back in the drawer, takes the ammo box out. Puts all the ammo in a satchel. Dad's initials, *O. S. J.* (S for Sutter), glint gold on the brown satchel. I gave it to him for his birthday last year.

Dad heads back out to the living room. Grabs a jacket and a baseball cap out of the front closet. The cap—Twins, of course—is one of mine. Dad doesn't wear baseball caps. Then he takes the keys to *my* car from the key-rack-shaped-like-a-key by the front door. Goes outside, starts up my Toyota, and drives off.

I pop into the passenger seat. Study his face, which sags with age and worry. But determination too; he's on a mission.

"Where are we going, Dad?" I ask out loud.

No response, of course. Just that grim, focused visage under-lit by the glow of the dashboard.

When I finally get my answer, I don't like it.

Dad takes a bumpy dirt road that leads down to the Logan. I know this road; it leads to prime make-out territory on the riverbank, obscured by tall buckthorn. It's Margo's and my "special spot," and I'm a little pissed that Dad's chosen it for his midnight ramble.

After he parks, we get out. Flashlight our way down to the water. Dad has the satchel; he throws the ammo, then the ammo box into the gurgling darkness. Then squints, to see if the river's swallowed his secrets. But he can't see a thing. He gets back into the car, turns around.

Okay, I think, *there's logic to this*. If it comes out that mom was packing on the night of June's murder, the police'll ask to see their ammo. (The police at present being sick Roy, boy wonder Lance, and my deluded girlfriend. But still, this thing could open wider. Sam's already mentioned hiring a PI; don't know if that's a bluff or not.)

So anyhow, Dad's protecting Mom. That's Dad-like. Not too weird.

But our next stop shakes my new confidence: the all-night Walmart in Norfolk. And what does Dad buy, baseball cap pulled low to shield him from security cameras? Good ol', all-American Walmart ammo. As opposed to the distinctive Russian variety.

(*Why exactly did you have Russian ammo, Dad?? Ex-KGB double agent, perhaps?* All very strange.)

As we drive back home, thoughts pinball around my brain. *He's protecting Mom by replacing weird ammo with normal ammo. Right?*

But there's something off about this new, investigation-obstructing Dad. And I find myself wondering: *Is he protecting Mom? Or himself?*

That's when a nagging thought that's been hiding behind all the others walks out and introduces itself. And that thought is: *Why was Dad home taking a shower when all the other parents were at Back-to-School Night?*

TWENTY-THREE

HANK

'm alone in my house.

Dad didn't say much on the drive back to the hospital. He's in his head now, analyzing, strategizing. We're so much alike. The only directive he gave me was to go stay at Delia's house. I protested but he insisted. Said he'd feel better knowing I'm not home alone. I knew even as I agreed to it that I was going to defy him. I didn't want to see anyone; I just wanted to go home and close the door.

But now, alone in the house, the familiar suddenly seems frightening. The orange and brown afghan my grandmother crocheted, draped on the back of the sofa. The Huskers football helmet mug on the coffee table. The drapes in the living room, cream against the blackness outside. It's such a horror movie set-up: the coziness right before the murderer bursts in.

I remember a ritual my dad and I performed every night after my mother died. I was so scared that whatever got my mom would get me. So Dad and I would walk through the entire house, check each room, each closet, each door and window lock. I think it made him feel better too.

I head down to the basement. Nothing there except more horror movie setup: sweet family things like ice skates, a badminton net, Christmas decorations.

I explore the upstairs, turning on lights and leaving them on. This is not the same without Dad here, even though I'm older. It's not a game anymore.

A pillow on a chair in my mom's old sewing room almost gives me a heart attack. When I turn the light on it glows bright pink and startles me. It's heart-shaped, embroidered with the words "Mothers are forever." I gave it to her on the Mother's Day before she died.

My mother taught me to sew that year. That's how I commune with her now: up here sewing, listening to her old CDs: REM, Sheryl Crow, Sugar Ray. It's nice. I feel her inside me when I sew, her hands guiding the fabric. It feels—at least for an hour or so—like maybe mothers really are forever.

Her books are shelved on the back wall. Austen, Cather, Steinbeck—Mom loved to read. Sometimes I allow myself to remember the sound of her voice, reading aloud to me at bedtime. Taking on the voices of the Cheshire Cat, Aslan the Lion, Dudley Dursley. Her dark hair hanging in a silky curtain until she'd shove it behind her ear, animatedly acting out a character.

Mom belonged to a book club. June and Emmie James were in it too. Sometimes Mom would host it here; I remember the tinselly laughter of the group floating up to my bedroom. I wanted to be a part of it.

I haven't read all her books yet, but I will. Sometimes I find her inside them.

The satin pillow looks garish in the overhead light, so I turn it off. Then sit down and just hug the pillow in the dark room.

What would it be like to hug my mom now, I wonder. Now that I'm bigger and she's older? Or would I ever hug her at all?

Would I just be a bratty, self-absorbed teenager, acting out against her, exasperating her?

God, I think, it would be so nice, so relaxing to be spoiled by life. To have both parents safe and sound. Everyone dreaming away together in our house on a moonlit night.

I'm up in the sewing room for a long time. Finally I go down to the kitchen to make some tea.

The cold is the first thing I notice: the back door's open. But more shocking, absolutely terrifying, is the man standing in the middle of the room. Gib Hawkins.

As we stare at each other, my brain trying to process his presence, it dawns on me: all the lights in the world, all the yellow chintz kitchen curtains, can't keep the horror movie out of the house.

There's no Tough Guy left in me; I just gasp. He speaks first.

"Where's your dad?" he snarls.

"In the hospital," I say, before I realize "upstairs" might have been a better answer.

He blinks; clearly this is information he didn't have.

"He had a heart attack," I offer.

Gib's jaw starts working as he mulls this over. Finally he says: "He gonna live?"

"Yes. Yes, I think so," I say politely, ever the good girl. Even when a madman has burst into my house.

"He better," he growls. "'Cause he's gotta find this killer."

It's ugly, the way he spits the words out, but my whole body relaxes. He's not here to kill me. He's just here to rail at the police chief.

"He will," I squeak.

"How?" Gib demands. "How's he gonna find the killer if he's laid up in the hospital?"

"He'll be out in a couple of days. Then he and his deputy will get to the bottom of this."

I shouldn't have mentioned Lance. He's not a convincing argument for skilled detective work.

Gib spits on the floor. "Shit," he says. "I'll do it myself."

And with that he turns to go.

I look at the glob of spit, glistening on the red kitchen tiles. Tiles my mother laid herself. And suddenly the Tough Guy's back.

"Next time," I say to Gib's back. "Ring the bell. Don't just walk into my house."

He wheels around, fixes me with that hollow stare. "Why not?" he asks. "You walked into mine."

His stare makes me wish I'd kept my mouth shut. I can see how deep the fury and despair goes in him. Just because he didn't kill June doesn't mean he's not dangerous.

I used to listen to his radio show after my mom died. I was absolutely sure he killed her; who better in town to cast in the role of a crazed murderer? I told Dad but he told me—he's always told me—it's not my job to solve Mom's murder.

Gib looks me over, up and down, then takes a parting shot: "A woman may not exercise authority over a man. She is to remain quiet. Timothy 2:12."

By the time he walks out, my knees are knocking.

I lock the door, turn on the yard light, sit down in a kitchen chair, and just repeat Hank's name over and over again.

TWENTY-FOUR

HANK

'm brooding about Dad. Trying to reconcile his late-night antics with the man I know: cheerful, solid family man/doctor Orrin James.

It makes sense, doesn't it? Protecting his grieving spouse, who's gone a little too far 'round the bend? Sure it does. Because I can't bring myself to consider a darker scenario.

To distract myself, I decide to check up on Lance, see how he's doing with June's computer. I know he lives above Marcy's. Or pretty much in it: he's always there, breakfast, lunch, and dinner. I don't know if they even charge him; the guy is everyone's stray dog.

The apartment I pop into looks like it belongs to a ten-year-old boy. Heavy on the superhero decor: Captain America, Iron Man, the Fantastic Four, Wolverine, etc., are represented everywhere. An Aquaman figure, Avengers video games, a Hulk mug. A large poster of a bad-ass-looking Thor, wielding his mighty hammer. Lance's place is a shrine to the naturally and supernaturally powerful. I don't check the bedroom, but my guess is Spiderman sheets.

God, I liked this town better when I didn't know how everyone lived.

Over on a coffee table is an Xbox console and controller, plus the box a Fortnite game came in. Great, if there's ever a zombie invasion of Lazarus, Lance has experience shooting them. Although I'm one to talk: I'm a ghost, so who's to say zombies aren't next?

Next to the coffee table, Lance himself is curled up on a couch staring into space. Wonderful—I'm glad he's taking this investigation seriously. He's listening to loud, dramatic music. I check the MP3 player on his bookcase: it's the soundtrack to *The Dark Knight*. Of course.

Also on the bookcase are some family pictures: Lance with his parents, I presume. Plain-faced prairie types, like their expressions were worn off by generations of Nebraska wind. Dad a little tougher looking, Mom a little softer.

There's Lance at high school graduation, kid Lance on a pony, Halloween Lance as Batman. Pretty normal stuff. In fact, on the good side of normal: young Lance has the look of a well-loved kid.

The books on the shelf are all comic books. Except for a Bible. I guess they don't make a comic book version of that.

As I look around, I'm struck by an absurd thought: Lance bringing a date back here. How many seconds would it take her to run for the door? I wonder if he's ever had a date. A *real* date, not a Wonder Woman fantasy.

When I turn around, I realize Lance isn't staring into space. He's staring at a computer on a desk across the room. I move closer: the image on the screen is a picture from a newspaper of a young boy playing baseball. I move closer and read the accompanying article. It's a short sports rundown about a Little League game in June 2000. The caption on the picture reads: *Lance Ritter homers to win it for the Chiefs.*

I'm immediately irritated. Lance is lying around re-living his Little League glory days when he's supposed to be checking June's search history.

Where is June's computer anyway? I look around the room and then realize it's in front of me. The Little League picture is on June's computer.

This is one of the moments when I really, really wish people could hear me. Because I want to ask Lance why the hell he's looking up an old Little League game on June's computer when he's supposed to be working.

I glare at him for a while, trying to will him to get up and do his job. What would people think, I wonder, if they knew a pissed-off ghost was glaring at them when they were alone?

I'm just about to leave when Lance finally gets up and crosses to the computer. He sits down and closes the file. Which is interesting, because I realize he's not online. The Little League article was a file on June's computer. *Huh.*

Now he stares at the document list. And stares. I move closer to see what he's looking at. Every file I can see starts with his name: *Lance on swim team. Lance's scout troop plants garden. Lance's graduation* and so on. All these hometown news clips about Lance... on June's computer.

I've been snooping to see if anyone in town had an unusual interest in June. Turns out *June* was preoccupied with *Lance.* Why? Why would she document his boyhood, all these mundane events that happened long before he came to work at the station? Long before *they met?*

I hear sniffles and realize Lance is crying. Staring at the screen, really blubbering, tears and snot, full on. Is he surprised and moved by her interest in him? Or racked with guilt?

As I ponder this spectacle, I hear a voice, soft at first, then louder. It's Margo, calling my name.

I pop over to Margo's house and find her sitting at the kitchen table, shaking. Scared.

I instinctively go to put my arms around her but they pass right through. So I just sit and listen as she tells me about a weird visit from Gib Hawkins. We go over every word he said, break it down, analyze it. She starts to calm down, but I make the call not to fill her in on everything I've seen today. It can wait till the morning. She needs to sleep.

We go up to her bedroom and lie down. One of the few upsides to limbo: I can sleep with my girlfriend whenever I want. I just can't touch her. But I talk to her, soothe her, get her feeling safe again. It feels good to both of us after this freak-ass day. I feel *close* to her again, whispering in the dark.

After she goes to sleep, I go over everything I learned, parsing out each detail. The story's in there somewhere, I just don't have it yet. Finally I just watch Margo sleep, which is perfection. Long dark hair on moon-drenched pillow, soft cheek, lips slightly parted. Until she frowns, murmurs distress, the first nightmare of the night encroaching. I soothe her, get her settled down again. Then watch over her until morning. That's what I'm here for.

TWENTY-FIVE

MARGO

t's Saturday, and I am not at the Changs' house like I promised my Dad. Instead I'm at home, making the same mistake I always make when I'm trying to figure something out: just sitting in a chair, feverishly firing mental neurons until my brain is a lump of scorched gray matter. *Who had motive and opportunity? Who wasn't at Back-to-School Night? Who hated June, and why would anyone hate June?* Circles and circles, but no answers.

No solutions come from stasis. Where did I get that from? Probably Dad. Sounds like a Dad thing. And I know it's true; it's only been two days since June's murder, and I can't possibly have enough clues yet to solve the case. And yet here I sit, grinding the gears of my pre-frontal cortex (thank you, ninth grade Biology). I'm occasionally distracted by a painting on our living room wall, of kids playing in a park. It's a good painting, but I kind of hate it: happy kids playing, innocent of any darkness in the world. Sure, you're happy *now*, playing kids. But my mom picked it out at a flea market, so up it stays. Anyhow, that's my rhythm this afternoon: figure this out, figure this out, hate the painting, figure this out.

I went to see Dad this morning and he actually looked worse than he did yesterday. I think last night's meeting really took it out of him. Plus they have him on some medication now that makes him a little foggy. So I just sat on his bed, held his hand and told him happy lies: *Mrs. Chang made us these amazing apple pumpkin pancakes this morning! And Mr. Chang taught me this cool card trick! I'd show you if I had a pack of cards!*

He just nodded and smiled vaguely. The man who promised the town he'd solve June's murder in two months doesn't look like he could work a TV remote right now. I think it was that bleary smile that sent me home to my current position on our old, brown leather easy chair, manically trying to find a solution in stasis. Because I have *got to figure this out.*

The doorbell rings; my body literally jumps a couple of inches off the chair. I take a breath, straighten my pre-frontal cortex and answer the door.

It's Delia; I immediately bear hug her. It's such a relief, such a balm to see her, in her John Lennon t-shirt and checkered Vans. And yet something's off. She doesn't quite hug me back the way you do when, well, your town's gutted from too much *death*, but at least you've got your best friend. She's stiff, not quite making eye contact, which knots up my stomach. *What now?* Did she find something out? Something I'm not going to want to hear?

I invite her in and she perches herself on the couch rather formally. The same couch where she once acted out the wacked scenario of a cat accidentally left in a washing machine, rolling and screeching as Hank and I fell off our seats, crying with laughter. And now she sits there like a church lady coming for tea, not quite looking at me.

"What's wrong?" I finally ask her. It sounds strange, considering that pretty much *everything* is wrong right now.

She hesitates: "I just…" Then finally looking at me: "I just feel like there's something you're not telling me.

My stomach somersaults. There's *so* much I'm not telling her and suddenly it feels *awful*. We've always told each other everything, so of course she knows I'm withholding information. I so want to spill it all: Hank, the truth about Carolyn and Ted, the weirdness of Lance-at-home. What am I afraid of, that she'll think I'm crazy? Delia knows me, knows my whole life, the entire Book of Margo.

Maybe I'm afraid that if I tell someone—anyone—about Hank, he'll disappear? That I'll pop the bubble? I've stepped into a new dimension these past few months and I don't know the rules. So I listen to my gut, which tells me to keep it to myself.

And yet, my gut allows, this is *Delia*, and I really want to share what I can with her. So I tell her about Dad, the town hall meeting, the eerie kitchen stand-off with Gib Psycho Hawkins.

As I talk I see her posture relax a little, but not all the way. She still has that guarded look in her eyes, and I *so* want to make that disappear.

"Delia," I say. "What *is* it?"

Now she takes a breath.

"Well," she says, clearly being delicate. "I've just been wondering: how did you know your dad had a heart attack?"

I blink three times, totally unprepared for this.

"Thursday night," she goes on. "The night of the murder. You came running over, said your dad had had a heart attack. He was down at the station. How did you know?"

It did not occur to me, in the midst of the emergency, that this was information I could not know. It was *Delia*, after all, who knows everything about my life. In that moment, I think I thought, *Of course Delia knows about Hank.*

I look into her eyes, weighing the risk of telling her the truth. I almost choke as I finally lie: "He texted me."

She tries to make sense of this. "Your dad texted you while he was having a heart attack?"

"That was just it," I counter. "He just texted a jumble of letters. I knew something was wrong."

So lame, but miraculously she accepts it. She believes me because I always tell her the truth. She relaxes fully now, the stiffness all gone. But I feel like crap. Little by little, everything I value—including my integrity—is slipping away.

Her face—her regular Delia face—brightens and she starts prattling on about a party tonight. Someone's parents are out of town, everyone's going, I *have* to go, etc.

I try to beg off but she insists. This is just what I need right now, she says, to get my mind off things. She touches my arm and her eyes are so kind, I have to say yes. I can't let her down any more than I already have.

TWENTY-SIX

HANK

Margo asked if I wanted to go to the party with her and Delia, which was sweet, but I said no. She should be able to go to a party without her dead boyfriend tagging along.

I don't really like the guy who's throwing the party anyhow. Corey Jensen, one of Boyd's Neanderthal JV football friends. I'm glad Boyd's on the team. He's found something on the football field, an identity apart from me. He's fast and tough; it's a place where he can be his silent, deadly self. But the other guys on the team are mostly loud, stupid jock clichés. There will literally be beer can flattening on foreheads tonight.

But after an hour or so of playing guitar alone at the theater I'm truly bored. The hieroglyphs on the walls are a good audience, but they don't talk. Playing to them gets old.

So I pop over to the Jensen place. I've never taken LSD, but there's something in the vibe at the party that feels like a bad trip. Sweet Jensen family photos on the hall walls and "Live Love Laugh!" placemats in the kitchen beam in contrast to the dull-eyed revel taking place. It's post-murder fall-out: lights are low, kids are drunk and stumbling already, smoke from cigarettes and other smokables murks the air.

The dining room is the house-party-gone-bad epicenter. The football oafs are gathered, egging on an uber-oaf who's standing on the dining room table, shirtless, howling along to a Kanye West song into his beer-can-as-microphone. I'm so glad I'm not (really) at this party.

Beyond this freak show I can see much making out in the living room. No shirts off there, just a lot of slobbering. Fun to do, icky to watch. And over to one side, sitting on the floor of the dining room, is my brother. Taking solace in many beers, judging from his slack-jawed countenance.

I feel bad for the kid; I wish I could take him home and give him a glass of water and a multi-vitamin (best preventive for a hangover). But then something gets his attention: his eyes sparkle, his jaw rights itself. I turn to see what it is and catch sight of Margo through the doorway to the kitchen. She's standing, chatting in a circle of relatively sober-looking girls, including Delia.

Boyd heaves himself up, crosses and plants himself in the kitchen doorway, balancing by holding on to both sides. Margo turns around and comes face-to-face with him. She greets him warmly but they're at two different parties: she's *not* hammered, just talking to a group of girls, and he's just emerged from a beer-soaked circle of Hell.

He asks if he can talk to her. Sure, she responds.

Okay, I think, maybe this is a good development. Maybe in this condition Boyd can finally get out how he's feeling.

Margo follows Boyd to a door that leads to a back deck. They go outside; I pop out along with them. It's chilly outside and quieter. The two of them are silhouetted by the slant of a single porch light. Boyd shoves his hands in his jeans, suddenly awkward despite all the liquid courage he's imbibed.

"I want to tell you..." he starts, then: "I want to tell you something."

"Of course," Margo encourages him. "You can tell me anything."

At this, Boyd stops fidgeting and just looks at her. He's always been a man of few words and it looks like he's trying to communicate what he wants to say with his eyes. And there's a lot in there: pain, intensity, and something else. Longing?

"I need…" he starts this time. And then suddenly he's cradling Margo's face in his hands and kissing her. And here's the main thing I notice: she doesn't immediately push him off. In fact, a good minute goes by before she steps away.

The look she gives him, tears in her eyes, is more sympathetic than angry.

"*No*, Boyd," she says. "I can't."

And with a last look she goes back into the party. Boyd looks down at his sneakers, swaying slightly in the autumn chill, and whispers, "I'm sorry" to no one. It's the loneliest sight in the world. I honestly don't know if I want to slug him or hug him.

TWENTY-SEVEN

MARGO

've been up all night talking to Hank. Hank did not love witnessing the kiss between me and Boyd, obviously, but by morning we've reached an agreement that, in his inebriated state, Boyd just wanted a *connection*—with me, with Hank, with *something*.

But deep down, underneath the surprise and sadness of it, the secret truth is that something about Boyd's kiss felt good too. I think it's partly because Boyd's a James, partly because he can actually touch me now and Hank can't. But the deeper, darker truth is that Boyd James is just stone sexy. And his lips on mine felt hot.

My shame at this makes me cry, and Hank's comforting words make me cry harder. I wish I could just curl up and sort out my feelings, just lay around the house all day. But I can't. June's funeral is today.

Hank pops out as I finally get up. It's time to get ready.

I look at the knee-length black dress with the cream lace Peter Pan collar (thrift store, of course) that I laid out on my desk last night. Suddenly it looks too cute. Should I dig for something else? A suit of armor maybe, to protect me from all harm and from all that I'm feeling?

Finally, I just put the stupid thing on, swearing at the difficult, ancient zipper.

I have to get my dad from the hospital. He has to go to the funeral—I get that—but I'm a wreck and I feel like I can't take worrying about him on top of everything else. I'm shaking as I drive into the hospital parking lot.

Dad looks a little better. He tells the nurses he's going home today and they don't argue. I feel relieved and terrified by the possibilities at the same time. What's the stress hormone? Cortisol? I feel like a cortisol time bomb by the time we pull up to the church.

Lance sees us in the back parking lot and tries to help Dad get out of the car. It would be a bit comical—Lance reaching for Dad's arm and Dad swatting him away—if I weren't looking at Lance with new eyes today. What exactly was he looking at on June's computer? Why was it so upsetting to him? And did he ever do his job and look further? I want to just ask him, but I can't with Dad there.

Dad insists on walking into the church on his own, no wheelchair. Lance and I flank him, just in case. We make our way around to the front.

A sad phalanx of mourners trudge into the church. A murder funeral is different than a regular funeral; the usual bleak torpor is infused with dread. People dart quick glances at each other: Was it *you?* They don't seem as welcoming to Dad as they were at the council meeting; it's as if his frailty is another blow.

Delia and her parents meet up with us by the church steps. Delia's worried about me; she knows something happened at the party. But I brush it off, don't tell her about the kiss. Delia's always had a thing for Boyd. It's a running joke that she swoons

over his hotness, but I think she really does like him. I don't
know if I'm protecting him or her by not telling her.

I see Delia purse her lips at my brush-off; she knows I'm
withholding again. Her mom, Zhen, comes over, an intense look
on her face. She clasps both my hands, a hint of violet eyeliner
making her gaze even more electric.

"I want you to know," she says, "*anything you need*, we're
here for you. Okay?"

Yes, I say, thanks. Then she turns the intensity up a notch,
squeezes my hands and says: "I'm watching out for you."

I want to cry. It's a mom, someone else's, letting me know
she will be my rock if I need one. And not just any mom: Zhen
Chang has always had what Delia and I call a *woo-woo* side.
Goes to card readers and seances, lights candles and communes
with her ancestors. So when she says she's watching out for me, I
know she means it not just literally, but spiritually. Which feels
even more powerful.

I want to hug her but don't. I just thank her again.

As we go inside, my dad whispers, "You didn't stay over
with them, did you?"

I just look down and keep going.

The first thing I see inside the church annoys me. The flowers on June's casket are pink and white. It's just so wrong: June
was not remotely a pink kind of woman. This is what happens
when there's no family around and all the friends are too flipped
out to take charge: you get some generically female flowers on
your coffin. She might as well be a Jane Doe. I think of June's
love of Mexican art and jewelry, the red and yellow-striped serape on the back of her couch. Her flowers should have been
brilliant and exotic. I know it's a minor thing, but I wish I'd been
on it.

Little by little the church fills up. I see Sam and Carolyn
Claypool in their funeral finery; Sam in a black suit with a subtle
purple pinstripe, Carolyn in a silky purple dress. It's too bad she

wants to run off with her lover; she and Sam make such a perfect, stylishly villainous pair. Surely this Louboutins-at-a-funeral woman wants the craven developer with a Porsche, not a high school teacher. Is she really going to be happy in their South Seas love nest, listening to him recite sonnets? Have you *really* thought it through, Carolyn?

But maybe she has. Maybe Hank's first suspicion was right and they're plotting more than a getaway. With a little toxic mixology, the chemistry teacher could get the house, the Porsche, *and* the handsome poet.

Between these grim musings and my confused feelings for Boyd, I suppose it's a good thing I'm in church today. As Gib would say, *repent!*

Gib and Ted arrive together. Gib is his usual Old Testament self: self-righteously stony-eyed and vengeful in an ancient black suit. Ted is tastefully outfitted in a trim gray suit. He has his sympathy face on, greeting his fellow mourners with soulful eyes. Could be genuine, could be a polished front—I never know with that guy.

Now Boyd arrives with his parents. Normally I'd be keeping an eye on Emmie, who doesn't look good: sleepless circles under her eyes, too thin in a plain black dress. But the sight of Boyd, awkward and hungover in a dark suit, confuses me. I can suddenly feel his lips on mine and this is the *wrong* place for that kind of feeling. He dares a look at me and I look away, blushing. I don't want to have a new kind of relationship with Hank's brother; it's too much on top of everything else.

It's somehow reassuring to see Al and Linda Nordgren arrive. Al's diner, Marcy's, has always been a warm, grilled-cheese-after-school town gathering place. Al looks a bit dour today, but then again he always does; his tall, lanky frame usually bent over swabbing tables, because the man can never stop working. His petite brunette wife Linda is a direct contrast to Al; Linda Nordgren, always smiling and welcoming people on the way into Marcy's, then offering mints (and M&Ms to us kids) and another smile on the way out. Today Linda looks put-together and actually kind of radiant in a nice, V-necked, A-line black dress and a sapphire necklace.

A sapphire necklace. With earrings to match.

This does not make sense.

I tell myself, *Well of course, they're not real sapphires. Probably a QVC knock-off.*

But I'm a jewelry girl; I've spent hours inspecting estate jewelry in vintage shops. And there's a certain distinct color and sheen that real sapphires have. And that's what's around Linda Nordgren's neck.

It's funny how your rational mind fights your instincts some-times. Rational Me is declaring that there's *no way* the Lazarus diner owner's wife is wearing real sapphires. But Instinctual Me is already exploring the possibilities: an inheritance, maybe? Or something darker, something June found out about?

As I stare at that deep blue necklace, another shade of blue comes to mind: *aqua.* The color of the new decor at Marcy's. And with that comes a question: how did Al Nordgren come up with the money to remodel his place this summer? Is there that much expendable income to be made running a small-town din-er?

Now a word arises in my mind amidst all these scurrying questions. And that word is *opportunity.* Motive's best buddy, when it comes to solving crimes. That word is ringing out be-cause I've just realized that Al Nordgren was the *literally the closest person* to June last Thursday night. He could have zipped across the street to the station and been back before anyone no-ticed. Plus he and his wife don't have kids, hence no reason to attend Back-to-School Night. Did June find something out about Al's sudden, mysterious windfall, something he didn't want any-one to know? I don't have a motive for him yet, but I realize I can move Al into first position on *opportunity.*

This new line of thought has to quiet down as the minister starts the ceremony. I'm appropriately attentive, but after the first ten minutes of the service, I realize that Reverend Foster's starting to bug me. His words are kind and appropriate, but I'm not sure how well he knew June. She was a churchgoer, but not one to head committees, man bazaars, and such. She was too busy at the station.

Couldn't he have asked around a bit more? Like, asked *me?* Gotten a better sense of who June was?

Anyhow, we're all limping through this sad ritual when suddenly a tidal wave crashes down on the ceremony in the form of Gib Hawkins.

For a minute or two before, he could be heard clucking and grumbling in his seat. A preacher himself, he clearly doesn't like the job Reverend Foster is doing. I can relate, I think, because I feel the same way.

But now, out of the blue, Gib leaps to his feet and shouts, *"This is a charade!"*

Everyone freezes and stares, including Reverend Foster. Ted turns paper white, an absolute statue.

"A *fraud* in the house of the Lord!" continues Gib, shouldering his way up to the altar.

Reverend Foster looks around for support, clearly not up to subduing this force of nature by himself. But everyone's still stunned, and Gib's just getting started. He claps a possessive hand on June's casket and glares out at the congregation, eyes raging, jaw quivering.

"Our sister in Christ has been *murdered!*" he bellows. "And not by some bandit passing through town. Nothing was taken. No, no—the serpent is *here in our own garden!*" He points a bony figure outward. *"She was slain by one of you!"*

I'm as shocked as everyone else but worried too; I can hear my dad starting to breathe heavily. He knows it's his job to stop this. I look at him: his clenches his jaw, trying to will his strength back. He starts to get up, then slumps back. Seeing his struggle wakes some of the other men up: Dr. James, Riley Kagan, and some of the other men make their way to the aisles.

"You must reveal yourself!!!" thunders Gib. "There is no escape for you now, no reprieve from the fiery furnace! *Reveal yourself*, or God will strike you down, as you smote my... my..." He's crying now, touching the casket.

It occurs to Ted, a little late, that he should be among the men trying to subdue his father. He starts to get up, then falters. Looks like he might faint.

Sam Claypool also realizes he should be helping and joins the men. It probably occurs to him that it's in his best political interests to help eject the madman from the church. Lance doesn't join in, which surprises me. He just sits there looking scared.

Riley and Dr. James reach Gib, but it takes more men to hustle him out of the church. As they drag him out, he keeps demanding a confession.

Reverend Foster continues the service, but the mood is irreparably damaged. There's no room now for gentle grief, just a return to the sickening emotional vigilance of a traumatized population. We murmur through a couple of hymns and then finally the funeral staggers to a conclusion.

I help my dad up; he looks shaken. I realize that in addition to everything else he's having an identity crisis: five civilians just did the job he's supposed to do. He looks stricken, helpless. I need to get him home.

A couple of my dad's friends see how unsteady he is and help him down the steps. I just want to get Dad the hell out of here, but as I reach the top of the steps, I see Lance. He's sitting midway down the steps, doubled over, sobbing.

I need to get Dad home, but I stop for a moment, put a hand on Lance's shoulder. He doesn't even notice.

But then a mental switch flips and I slowly, carefully, take my hand back. Because suddenly I'm not sure if I'm comforting a grieving friend or a guilty murderer.

TWENTY-EIGHT

HANK

'm watching my brother eat lunch. Seated across from him at our dining room table. Maybe I'm obsessing, but I want to get a good look at the guy who kissed my girlfriend last night. The guy who happens to be my brother.

Boyd's eating a big overstuffed sandwich that my mom has made him. Pickles, chips. I notice there are three placemats on the table now, not four. I actually find this encouraging; the fourth family member *isn't coming back*. But there's a dreariness in the house that I don't remember from my mortal days. Faint light filtering in through drawn curtains. Gloom.

I really study my brother, something I haven't done, well, ever that I can remember. He has the wide jaw of a predator, pounding down that big sandwich like it was a Twinkie. But maybe that's just how I see him today: a predator after my girl.

My mom, still in her black dress, brings out watermelon slices; he doesn't even nod thanks. A strong feeling of animosity is pouring out of me and beaming straight at my brother. But why, really? It's just my kid brother eating a sandwich. Is it all because of one *extremely* drunken kiss?

I watch him pause momentarily to smooth his hair before he goes to work on the watermelon. Wavy brown hair. Long-lashed brown eyes. So different than my funny-guy-with- little-blue-eyes-behind-glasses look.

Boyd's a stud, or looks like one, anyhow. Girls will swoon over him and he'll finish high school and go to college, maybe on a football scholarship. Then go to work—maybe medicine like Dad—then pick out a pretty girl to marry, have some kids. And then maybe Mom'll finally be happy again, playing with Boyd's long-lashed kids. And I realize: *That's why I hate him. Just because he's alive.*

My mother brings in a salad. This is unusual, and Boyd squints at it, confused. Says: "That's okay, mom, I don't really need a…"

But she's gone again. Boyd looks at the salad. Within minutes Mom's back, this time with a green bowl of grapefruit pieces and a plate of sliced cheese and crackers. This is getting odd; I happen to know my brother doesn't like grapefruit. So does Mom.

Boyd protests: "I really don't need all this, Mom. I'm full."

At first she's a sweet TV mom: "You need to eat, honey. You don't look good." The guy does look a little ashy. He's hungover, after all.

"It's okay, really—"

"But with football and everything," she insists, "you need to stay healthy."

Boyd pushes away from the table, as if to make his point. "I'm healthy, Mom. I'm good."

Sweet TV Mom is gone in a flash: *"You need to stay healthy!"* she yells. Boyd freezes, not sure what he's dealing with here. Mom goes on, sputtering: "You need fruits and vegetables and protein at *every* meal. You're still growing and you *need to stay healthy!"*

Boyd's not one to be pushed. He casts a steady eye at her. "I've had enough, Mom. I'm *done.*"

Mom stares at him. It's not a mom stare, it's clinical. Appraising.

"Who are you?" she says, finally. This jolts Boyd. Me too.

"What do you mean? I'm Boyd."

"Yeah, but who *are* you?" she continues in the same ice water voice. "You just skulk around here. You don't talk, you don't laugh, you don't have friends over."

Oh crap. She's dunning him for not being me. I see Boyd getting younger by the minute, shrugging helplessly.

"I don't know, I've got a lot of work for school, I've got practice…"

Mom continues her assessment: "Always on your computer, off to football, in the shower. You're like a locked door. I don't even know who's behind there."

Now would be the time—in a Lifetime movie, anyhow—for Boyd to say: "I'm grieving, Mom. I'm messed up by Hank's death and I know you are too." And then they'd hug and cry and bond. But *because* they're messed up, that's not what happens.

"I'm sorry I'm not Hank," Boyd spits out, and then bounds up the stairs. Mom stares at the dishes on the table for a minute, then quietly starts to clean up.

It's *so sad* that I can't watch either of them anymore, so I pop into the next room. My dad's study. I stretch out in his reclined leather reading chair. I'm so wiped by my *roadkill* of a family that I need to recover.

Despite his late-night adventures, there's something reassuring about Dad's study: medical books neatly shelved, his AMA journals thoroughly skimmed and flagged for points of interest. I see he's been reading psychiatric books, which is not surprising. I'm sure he thinks he can figure Mom's deal out and get her back on track. But honestly, I wish he'd just get her to a good shrink in Omaha. Someone she can really work this out with. But the whole Doctor Who Thinks He's God thing is not a myth, so I'm sure Dad thinks he can fix this himself. He's obsessed with healing people, and I get it: his family died in a fire, back in Texas. He was nine and staying overnight at a friend's house the night it happened. In one night, his mom, dad, and sister were just *erased* from his life. So that's why he'd crawl through a minefield to save Mom, his great love, who filled in the hole where his family used to be.

I spot a half-empty bottle of scotch and a glass on a cabinet near his desk—that's new. Dad's generally not a big drinker, though he can get a little cheerful sometimes at summer barbecues. "After all, I'm a Texas boy," he'll say, hitting the twang hard.

So now he's drowning his troubles in here old school, and who can blame him? The troubles have definitely been piling up.

I look out the French doors at our driveway basketball half-court. A real pang in the chest at this; the James men had some great times out there. First my dad teaching us—two little squirts, dribbling the ball into our faces half the time. Then gradually getting good enough to actually play, kids against Dad. Boyd and I both dying to show off for him. My dad's an athlete—he lettered in basketball, football, and baseball in high school—but he'd go easy on us, playing along at our speed.

I can still *feel* it, still hear it: the sweat flying, the *thoing* of the ball on asphalt. The ultimate thrill of a perfect three-pointer. We'd get into a rhythm: one dribbling low, one reaching wide, the pass, the shot. Like a single organism. A *team*. We were all *so alive*. And now none of us are.

TWENTY-NINE

MARGO

Dr. James insisted on coming home with Dad and me to help get Dad settled in. I knew Dr. James wasn't happy that Dad wanted to come home so soon and now, downstairs getting Dad water, I can hear them arguing upstairs. I creep up the steps and eavesdrop for a minute. Dr. James is chastising Dad for leaving the hospital—he should have stayed at least a week. Dad's forcing his cheerful voice, insisting he's fine. Saying that getting back to work will be the best thing for him. Dr. J comes back hard: *Do you want to leave Margo alone?* No response. Dr. J goes on: what Dad needs is to follow his release protocol and *rest*.

I knock and push the door open; both men put on strained smiles for me. Dad's propped up in bed, looks spent. As I give him his water he manages a wisecrack, deadpanning: "Marg, can you bring me my teddy bear? Doc James says I have to stay in bed."

Dr. James sighs and says he's turning Dad over to me. He shows me Dad's meds list, prescribes a healthy diet that makes

Dad groan. Says Dad can start taking walks next week, but *slow* and only a couple of blocks.

"Can I still do the Shriners' Circus next week?" mocks Dad. "I'm their only trapeze guy."

Dr. James frowns at him. "I would tell you to try yoga but I know you'd laugh me out of here."

"True," says Dad.

Dr. James shoots Dad his toughest look. "My number one warning, Roy Pierce, is that you should not go back to work for at least a month."

"Great," says Dad, just as tough. "It's not like there's much going on anyway."

One last tense stare between them. If they were bulls, they'd be pawing the earth. Dr. James breaks it, turns to me.

"Margo, I'm counting on you to keep him on his regimen. Okay?"

"Don't worry, I can handle him," I bluff. Dr. James just nods and heads downstairs.

I turn to Dad, who sits up straighter but doesn't try to get out of bed. "Now," he says, all business, "where the hell is Lance? I've called him twice and he didn't pick up."

I tell him Lance is still upset about the funeral, that he's having a tough time. Dad sniffs at this.

"Other people get to be upset," he says. "Police officers get to work."

He does not look like a guy who should be getting to work. Which is why I ask him again if I can pack up June's house. There have to be some answers there. "After all," I note, "she doesn't seem to have any family. I want to do this for her."

Even with his face pale and veined, Dad manages to fix me with an intimidating look. "Whoever did this to June hates me. He killed my secretary and may have killed my wife too. So who's next? Who do I love more than anything in this world?"

It's a rhetorical question; I don't answer.

"If I could I'd lock you in a tower and bury the key until I get this guy," he continues. "But I can't, so the best I can do is make sure you have *no involvement whatsoever in this case*. Got it?"

I nod but can't help but venture: "But who is this guy? And if he hates you that much, why June and not me?"

Dad answers before he remembers I'm shut out of the case. "June was trying to stop his development. She had a whole presentation and petition ready for the town council meeting."

Sam Claypool—of course. The obsession continues. But Dad's right, that *is* a motive. I just don't know if Sam is that ruthless. I need to find out more.

I tell Dad he needs to get some rest but he's already firing up his laptop. Oh well, I figure, at least he's in bed. I head downstairs and am surprised to find Dr. James is still there, waiting for me in the living room.

He repeats that Dad has to take it easy, and I'm touched that he's so worried about his old friend. But then he goes deeper, talking to me like an adult for the first time in all the years I've known him. He says he thinks my mom's death weakened Dad's heart. And that he's gained weight because he stopped caring about his health after she passed. He goes on to warn me about other possible blowback after someone has an MI (myocardial infarction—I heard that enough times in the hospital that it's branded on my brain).

"It's like a form of grief in itself," he says. "There may be anxiety, denial, even depression. So just talk with him, keep an eye on him. This is your job now, taking care of your father. Because nothing's more important than family, right?"

I look into his eyes, as sky blue as Hank's, and suddenly I see the boy in him. The lost little boy whose whole family died in a fire. *There's nothing more important than family.* Of course, that's why he wanted to talk to me. We're all trying to heal something; some more than others.

"Don't worry," I say. "I'll take care of him."

"And yourself too, Margo," he adds. "That's important too." For emphasis he takes one of my hands and squeezes it. And with a sad smile he heads for the door. I should walk him out but I'm too busy fighting back tears.

As he walks down the porch steps I think, *I will take care of Dad. I will take care of myself,* whatever that means. But I will also take care of June. Because if not me, who?

THIRTY

HANK

I promised Margo I'd check in on the Nordgrens, so I do. I told her I think she's off about them, but when I pop over to their house, I'm not so sure.

For starters, the mocha leather sectional couch (with recliners) looks new. Very un-Nordgreny. But more important is the marital argument I hear going on in the kitchen. I pop in there.

First impression: no fancy new appliances or anything, just a cramped, pale yellow, 1950s-looking galley kitchen. Second impression: the way Al is leaning over his wife looks menacing.

He's berating Linda for something; she's defending herself. As the spat continues, I realize it's about *jewelry*; Al thinks his wife shouldn't have worn the necklace Margo mentioned in public.

"Well then why did you say I could get them if I can't wear them out?!" counters Linda, clutching her necklace. I don't know jewelry but they look like real gemstones.

"Because I didn't think you'd be dumb enough to wear them in front of the *whole town!*" Al harangues. Wow. I've never seen

this side of Al. He's always just been part of the Lazarus landscape, usually manning the register at Marcy's. Solicitous,
hardworking. Proud, I always thought, of his pretty wife. But
now he's letting her have it.

"I told you when it happened: *no one must know!* And here
you go parading our secret in front of everyone!"

When it happened. No one must know our secret. Yeah,
there's definitely something going on here.

Linda's crying now, stroking her jewels. Then, slowly, sulki-
ly, she takes the necklace off. Then the earrings. But she's not
just sulking, she's pissed. She spits at Al: "Fine! I'll take them
back!" She throws the jewelry on the kitchen counter, storms into
the master bedroom, slams the door shut.

As Al stares at the bright blue jewels on the counter, I try to
read his expression. Angry still, but also guilty? It's hard to say.
Al would be a good poker player.

I stand there for too long, watching him. Because I want a
rewind on this one; I don't want to suspect Al Nordgren of murder. And I really, *really* don't want to have *been* murdered. I
want to be swinging into Marcy's with Margo on a Friday night,
ordering a big plate of cheese fries. (American cheese melted on
fries. Trust me, the disgusting/rewarding ratio weighs in favor of
rewarding.) I want to come in from the cold with my girlfriend,
pink-cheeked, innocent of any undercurrent of malevolence in
my town. I also want to not hate my brother.

I want to come in from the cold.

But no rewind happens; Al stares at the precious gems on his
worn kitchen counter and I pop the hell out of there. Lean back
against the lobby wall in the Egyptian and play a woeful tune on
a violin.

THIRTY-ONE

MARGO

Monday.

I think some of the kids at school have been told by their parents to avoid me. My friends offer concern and support, hugging me and asking me about Dad. But kids I don't know as well look genuinely scared of me as they scurry by. It's all so weird.

But really, I can't blame them. I'm the girl whose mother, boyfriend, and father's secretary have all died violently. I wouldn't get too close to me either.

One good sign: I didn't care what I wore today. I just threw something on. I think I'm ready to finally ready to *do* this detective job, not just dress for it.

I can't concentrate on my classes. My mind is still processing and re-processing everything Hank told me this weekend. Seems like everyone in town has a secret, including *Lance*, of all people. What is this connection between June and Lance, and why did I never notice it before? Did she have something on him he needed to silence?

And then there's my Black Widow chem teacher. I'm starting to think Hank's mom is right about her. But how can I tell my dad she's up to something?

This is the kink in Hank's and my PI partnership—how can I act on information he gathers?

And now I'm facing another suspect, Ted Hawkins. I'm in English class, spacing out as he blathers on about *Hamlet*, which I was supposed to read over the summer but didn't.

I can't follow what he's saying: *Hamlet's father's a ghost... Ophelia goes mad... Hamlet and Laertes duel...*

All I can think is, *You tried to stop your father from looking for June's killer. Why would you do that unless you're guilty?*

I'm trying not to make eye contact with him but he keeps catching me. It's like he's trying to beam his professorial charm at me in particular. Me, who he didn't want in his house.

After class, I try to hustle out but he stops me. Says he wants to talk to me. I feel my throat close up as all the other kids file out.

When we're alone, he sits on the edge of his desk. I keep a student desk between us. But the look on his face surprises me: not the Cool Teacher, not the Charmer, but genuinely sympathetic.

"How are you doing?" he asks. "With everything going on?"

I tell him I'm okay. He asks about Dad and I give my stock answer: he's doing better but not 100 percent yet. I'm not ready to give him any information about my family.

He looks down, takes a breath, then says: "The thing is... I went through hell when I was a kid too. It's a *bitch*, dealing with all that when you're just a kid. And certainly no young person deserves as many knocks as you've had."

I almost gasp. I search his face: there's no trace of artifice. Just a fellow survivor, reaching out.

"Thanks," I stutter.

Is it possible I've been wrong about him? That his smooth persona emerged out of the same crapstorm I've been through?

"Also," he continues. "I've been wanting to ask you something. What would you think about joining the school paper?"

I'm so surprised I almost laugh. He goes on that he likes the way I write, likes my "specificity of language," my journalistic style.

As he talks, my heart starts pounding. Because he's asking me to take over for Hank. And that's so *truly cool* that I want to cry.

"Yes," I blurt, cutting him off.

His face brightens; we both laugh. And damned if there's not a moment of heart-to-heart connection between me and the English teacher.

THIRTY-TWO

HANK

've firmly compartmentalized my anger at Boyd. Because the kid's a mess. He was a mess all summer; he hasn't been himself since I died. Plus he was drunk, which normally I don't accept as an excuse for anything, but in this case... I'll allow it. He wanted something from Margo, but not the obvious. Help, I think. Some kind of *relief*, or maybe just to feel *alive* again. I can relate to that.

So my mind's returned to its pre-kiss state, ready to help Margo.

I've been out spying on the Macs today and have some news for her. Can't get much of a read on the McLeans—they seem like typical Lazarus parents. He works at some soul-killing office job and she both works out a lot and eats a lot of snack foods. The MacAllisters were even more boring: reading, petting the dog, watching reality shows on TLC. Not much there. But the surprise that I weirdly enjoyed was my visit to Mrs. McNamara's. Widowed, sweet as the day is long, ex-president of the Lazarus Garden Club. Her house was a quintessential retired

Sunday School teacher's home: antiques with lace doilies, framed watercolors on the walls, a knitting project on the couch. Mrs. Mac herself, a bit stooped now, watering her plants outside, then inside, then in her little greenhouse out back, which has lovely, thriving potted ferns and flowers and *holy crap, about twelve pot plants!* Hah! Not that I partake, but I know buddage when I see it. Well, well, Mrs. Mac, that's certainly one way to while away the retirement hours.

But then the creepy part walked in the door.

"Hi Danny!" Mrs. Mac called out from the greenhouse. Danny—thirties, a big, sullen lug of a guy (and her son, I'm guessing)—barely murmured hello before trudging upstairs. And here's the creepy part; I can't eat any more but I can smell, and Danny McNamara smelled like *death.* I can't explain it but I know what death smells like—maybe from my own—and it was all over Mac Junior. So much so that I hightailed it back to the theater, spied out and creeped out. But then remembering why I'd gone spying on the Macs in the first place: June's note. Pot is still illegal in Nebraska, either recreational or medicinal. Was Mrs. Mac growing the stuff for a little extra income, then having Danny distribute it? And then, what, *killing* his customers once they paid him?

Okay, all of that might be a bit of a reach, but still, she's got a fair amount of weed growing back there and the smell on Dan was undeniable. I wish I could still take showers.

It was nice to get back to the Egyptian after that weirdness. It's peaceful, and it feels like *my* place. After spending so much time in strange domiciles, it's nice to have a haven.

And then I realize it's *not* entirely peaceful: I can hear voices coming from inside the theater. Strange; the troubled souls that flicker through here usually don't speak. I instantly feel put out, like I suddenly have noisy roommates. I push open the door to the theater.

I've never been in the actual theater before. The design continues the Egyptian theme: hieroglyphs, a mural of slaves carrying Cleopatra on a bower, the blue Nile. It's kitschy, but also kind of amazing: a gilded 1930s movie palace version of ancient Egypt.

Even more amazing is what's on the screen. It looks like a hidden camera video of Roy Pierce's bedroom. Roy's sitting up in bed talking to Lance. I take a few steps closer, mystified, as Roy and Lance discuss the investigation. Lance is telling him he didn't find much of interest on June's computer.

Sure. Nothing but a boatload of docs about *him.*

It's funny how when there's video anywhere, you get sucked into it, no matter where you are. So it takes me a minute to realize I'm not the only one in the theater.

There's a woman seated right in the middle of the auditorium watching the screen. I feel a kind of etiquette confusion, like I shouldn't interrupt her while she's watching the movie. So I just stand there, watching along with her. Surprised by Lance's talent for lying.

Roy seems to be accepting Lance's report at face value, nodding, assessing. Finally he tells Lance he's got an assignment for him: tail Sam Claypool. Be discreet but stay on him. Do whatever you have to do.

Of course Roy would single out his lifelong nemesis first. But I think he's off on this one. I think Sam's on his way to becoming another victim, not a perpetrator.

As Lance leaves Roy's room, the lights in the theater come up. The movie's over.

Over in her seat, the woman—who looks to be in her late 50s—sits thinking. I clear my throat; she turns around.

"Hi," I venture.

She greets me politely, seemingly unsurprised. She's shimmering a bit but in a different way than most of the specters I see in the lobby. Lighter, with more dazzling flecks of color.

I walk to the row in front of her and kneel on a seat. When I get a look at her—plain but pleasant face—I think, *I know her.* But from where?

I introduce myself, awkwardly adding, "I died in July." It seems like appropriate social protocol.

She says she's Alice Ritter. *Of course*, I realize. *Lance's mom.*

I ask if she's just passed and she says no, she and Lance's father have been gone for several years. When I ask why I haven't seen her before, Alice says she's been in "After." She came back because she saw June arrive over there. When I puzzle over this, she explains that she had entrusted June to look after Lance. So now that June's passed, she plans to periodically come back to the theater to check up on him.

So that's what the theater is. My mind whirs. A kind of hidden camera stake-out for the departed to check up on loved ones.

When I ask why she doesn't just pop back down among the living, she answers, "Oh, we can't do that anymore."

She asks if I do that—walk among the living. I tell her yes, in fact, I can still talk to one of them. At this Alice looks excited. If I can talk to the living, could I get a message to Lance?

I try to explain that I can only talk to Margo, but she's so elated, I hate to let her down. I tell her I'll try, and ask what she'd like me to say. Alice starts to cry, glittering tear crystals falling on her brown sweater.

"That I love him, of course," she says. "That I'm watching out for him."

At this, I want to cry myself.

I gingerly bring up my own concern about Lance. He's supposed to be investigating June's death, but I think he's hiding something. Would she have any idea why?

"I can't think why," Alice replies. "Lance loved June. After all, she gave birth to him. He doesn't know that, but I think he feels she's special."

At this, I actually fall off my perch on the seat and have to re-position myself. "June was Lance's *mother?*"

"Well, *I'm* his mother," Alice counters. "We adopted him. June was a young woman in a predicament and had to give him up. Which turned out to be our good luck."

There's so much I want to ask her: Who was the father? Was it Gib? How did she "entrust" Lance to June? Does she know who murdered her? And what is "After" like?

But she's starting to shimmer. Alice says she needs to get going; she can't stay down here long. She doesn't want him to notice she's gone. I don't know if she means the big Him—who presumably knows all—or Lance's father. She starts to disappear.

"Wait!" I protest, my head exploding with questions. "How did you die?"

"Plane crash," Alice answers with a sad smile. Then adds: "You'll remember, right? To get my message to Lance?"

"Absolutely!" I say as she disappears altogether. And then I'm alone again, with a truckload of unanswered questions.

THIRTY-THREE

MARGO

My police work for tonight, ironically, involves breaking and entering. Specifically, into Lance's apartment. Sorry Lance, but I just don't believe there was "nothing of interest" on June's computer. And since he won't let me in to look at said computer, I'll have to take the computer *out*. Or it's hard drive, at least; better to leave the box. Odds are, Lance won't notice the drive's missing.

I've been sitting in my car in Marcy's parking lot for fifteen minutes now, waiting for Hank to pop in. It's getting darker earlier now, which is helpful to my cause, but a bit scary too. Shadows play across the gravel, elm trees sway as a lone streetlight comes on, illuminating the brightest thing in the parking lot: a brand-new-looking Dodge Durango, parked in the owner's parking space. Silver, perfect, almost sparkling in the streetlight's candescence.

As I take it in, my heart sinks. Looks like Al Nordgren bought a new car this year. Along with remodeling his restaurant and buying his wife sapphire jewelry. But *how?!* How is pragmatic, flinty Al suddenly throwing money around?

I had stopped into Marcy's this afternoon to ask Al if he could remember seeing anyone going into the police station the night June was murdered. After all, he was the only one downtown that night, and right across the street from the station. I watched him closely as he shook his head no: he did look a little guilty. But it *seemed* like guilt for not being more watchful, not having anything for me. If he was guilty with a capital G, I think he would have frozen, become defensive. That's how Dad says it usually plays out when you've snared the perp. But who knows for sure? This is my first case.

I need to dig into the Nordgrens more, but I can't wait any longer on tonight's mission. Hank was supposed to help me, with both getting the drive out safely and watching for Lance. But Lance is having dinner at Marcy's right now; I can't wait anymore.

Getting into his place isn't hard. I jog up the rusted iron back steps and angle myself into an open window a couple of feet from the back door landing. I wriggle in and plop down into the kitchen area of the odd cartoon hero lair that Hank described. There's no time to take it all in. I cross to Lance's desk; Hank said that's where June's computer should be. But it's not there. Just Lance's tablet.

A flash of panic. Did he destroy it? Chuck it in the river? And if so, how suspicious is *that?*

I dart around the apartment, manically looking in cabinets, under the couch, in the linen closet. And finally find it, in Lance's bedroom closet. It has a blanket over it, like a bad dog that's been caged and covered. Very strange.

I gently lift the blanket off, trying to memorize its exact drape for later.

I have no trouble getting the drive out. I've brought a screwdriver but I don't need it. Just a pinch release and the cover's off.

I carefully lift the drive out. The real challenge is getting the front cover back on. *How hard can it be to just reverse the process?* But it is.

On an ordinary evening, this would just be annoying. But tonight's not ordinary: I no longer trust Lance and he'll be coming home any minute.

Where the hell is Hank?! He was supposed to be my lookout. *What could be more important than this?!*

I'm out of time. I ram the cover back into place as best I can, but it's smudged and bent. Definite evidence of tampering. Too bad—I throw the blanket back on, close the closet door.

I'm bee-lining back to the window, clutching the hard drive, when something stops me. A picture of my mother, attached to Lance's fridge with a magnet. Mom—bright smile, warm, dark eyes. She's in our backyard, wearing a black summer dress with a lavender flower print. I remember that dress.

The image knocks the breath out of me. I stand there in Lance's kitchen, gazing at her. I don't like to be surprised by pictures of my mother. It takes too much out of me.

But I get it—Mom made him dinner every Sunday night, stepped in for his late mother. Of course he misses her too. So it's both touching and a little weird. Or maybe just unexpected.

Footsteps on the inside stairs bring me back to the present situation. I lope two clumsy steps and practically dive out the kitchen window. Swing an arm over and manage to catch the landing railing. But I can't find a foothold. My feet flail like Wile E. Coyote after he's gone off the cliff.

As I grab for security, my hand *launches* the hard drive high into the sky like an unintentional Hail Mary pass, disappearing into the night. I hear it thud somewhere across the parking lot.

I drop to the ground ten feet below, my feet *thwack*ing the hard pavement. Now I limp-run crazily in circles around the lot, searching for the hard drive in the dark. *Crunch.* Found it.

Back in my car, I feel the contours of the smashed drive, as if I can shape it back into working order. Great job there, Nancy Drew. You got the evidence and destroyed it at the same time.

When Hank pops into the passenger seat, I'm too rattled to yell at him.

"Thanks a lot" is all I say.

He apologizes, then explains what he just learned: *June was Lance's real mother*.

As I try to absorb this, a light goes on in Lance's apartment. Looking up at the yellow glow, I'm on mother overload. Hank just talked to Lance's mother, but June is his *real* mother. *My* mother's on Lance's fridge.

I hug June's hard drive harder, willing June to tell me what all this means.

THIRTY-FOUR

HANK

found out why Dan McNamara smells like death. I got in the car with the guy on his way to work, which was a bit of an ordeal in itself. Danny Mac likes the *worst* music—death metal, bad rap—anything howling, atonal, and violent. Plus he sings along, "sings" being a pretty loose description; you can't exactly croon along with that type of music.

I noticed a tattoo on his right arm of a skull with a snake writhing out of one eye socket, capping the head and then hissing from the center front forehead. *Okaaay.* I studied his face: meaty, pale, angry. Ol' Danny definitely has some issues. He may or may not be the local dope dealer, but he definitely looks like a guy who could kill someone.

Dan pulled into a large compound simply called JB Plant, showing his badge to a guard at the gate. Then I followed him into a big, sterile room with gray metal lockers and benches, where he and a couple of other guys put on their work gear: white coat, hair nets, ear plugs, hard hats, and thick yellow gloves. From there they picked up tool kits and crossed to a door marked "Production Floor." One of the other guys punched in a code, which opened the door. They entered single file, Dan at the rear.

The first thing I noticed about the production floor—a huge room—was that the actual floor was painted red. Then the noise: partially coming from two conveyor belts humming as they brought slabs of something to the men assembled around the belts. And partially the flat, eerie *thwack* of metal on metal. The third thing I noticed was the temperature: a good twenty degrees colder than in the adjoining room.

As Danny crossed to take his place at the belt, a guy turned to greet him, and here's where my attitude went from curiosity to revulsion. Because the guy's white coat was covered in blood: blood spatter, patches of slick, drippy blood, smudges of caked dry blood. As a greeting, he held up his work tool, a knife long and sharp enough to resemble a sword. Danny took out his and *clanged* the other guy's, like two knights celebrating a particularly gruesome battle.

Looking down at the floor, I realized why it was painted red: to camouflage all the blood splashes.

Okay, I thought to myself, so Danny works in *Hell*.

Upon closer inspection, I realized that the slabs coming down the conveyor belt were chunks of meat. Dan took his place and got to work hacking off excess fat and gristle, letting it fall where it may. A meat-packing plant; that explains the death smell on Danny.

The whole scene was repulsive, though I know that makes me a hypocrite. I always enjoyed a good burger when I was alive, and I knew it had to come from somewhere. But the thing that really disturbed me was the change in Dan's face once he got to work. He actually looked *peaceful*, hacking away at something that was alive not long ago. He was meant for this; he clearly *enjoyed* it.

Dan McNamara, the Dark Prince of the Slaughterhouse.

THIRTY-FIVE

MARGO

After school Tuesday, I know I should get home to check on Dad. He keeps getting out of bed to try to accomplish something, then getting winded. We have this absurd routine going on in which I find him downstairs, chew him out, then herd him back to the stairs and slowly help him back into bed. Over and over; he's just not one for taking it easy.

I'll get home as soon as I can; I have a couple of stops to make.

I've packed up June's damaged hard drive and am overnighting it to a place called Cyber Salvage in Omaha. Given the condition of the drive, I don't have high hopes, but maybe they can find something on it. I take a breath as my turn comes up with Wendy, the ruddy-faced, curly-gray-haired post office lady. She likes to tell funny stories about her late husband. I get it, it's how she keeps him alive, but I just don't have time for that today.

But when it's my turn, I get the now-classic sympathetic look from her instead of a funny tale. She asks after Dad; I don't tell her that he's a pajama'd, would-be escape artist, and that I worry about his heart every minute I'm at school. I give her one of my standard lines and I'm out.

Across the street to the police station, which is now manned by a single employee: Lance Ritter. I have news for him, truths encased in lies, but what I'm looking for is his reaction. *Catch 'em off-guard and see the truth on their face*, Dad would say. But I'm not Dad and I don't want to catch him *too* off-guard with the delicate information I'm planning to convey. I was up a lot of the night (what else is new) concocting a story for him. First, I want to share his adoptive mother's message; he deserves that. But since I got it from Hank, and Hank's dead to everyone but me, I've decided to tell him that I went to a psychic looking for answers on June's murder. That a spirit came through, his mother Alice, with a sweet message for him. Then I'll ease into the truth about his birth mother. *That's* the reaction I want to see.

I've been mentally practicing my story all day, but when I get to the station I'm thrown off. The lights are on but Lance isn't at his desk. Fine, he's working at home, or *not* working at home, but either way, he should have closed up the station.

I'm about to call him when I hear noises from the back room. Dad's office.

I cross back there and open the door. And find Lance at Dad's desk, going through his papers.

Something about this enrages me; why the hell is he going through Dad's stuff?! Okay, maybe he's doing some kind of police work, but it infuriates me just the same, this incompetent lunkhead rifling through Dad's files.

My sweet fairy tale about the psychic goes out the window; I flat out ask him what he's doing. He looks at me dully, the light from Dad's brass desk lamp casting a diagonal line of shadow across the top of his face. He utters a single word: *working*.

Working. At a desk too big for him. At a job *way* too big for him.

That one word, plus the sight of this overgrown kid contaminating my father's files, floods me with all the backed-up rage of the past couple of months. I want to *hurt* him, point blank. So I blurt:

"I found out that June was your biological mother. Your 'parents' adopted you. Did you know that?"

I haven't even bothered with the lie I rehearsed, that I found his birth certificate among June's things.

His response is pure shock. His body appears to shrink in Dad's big, gray chair as he forms the soft word: "*No.*"

I'm shaking now, my anger morphing straight into guilt for this *fiery dart of the wicked* I've just thrown at him. This wasn't the way it was supposed to go down. And this poor schmuck was never meant for police work.

I've shattered him, I realize. He's found and lost his real mother all in one moment. Way to go, Margo.

I should sit down with him, talk it out, I *know* I should.

But I'm too ashamed.

"I'm sorry," I whisper. Then turn and hurry out the door.

THIRTY-SIX

HANK

I've been playing acoustic guitar at the Egyptian for a while, trying to mellow out, to get the sights and smells of JBs out of my mind. But it's not working, so I pop over to the James house.

Sadly there's no comfort here either. I sit with my family through their near-silent dinner, then follow my dad into his study. I watch him refill his scotch glass until he's gone from Dr. Calm to mad scientist, obsessively poring over his books. The effect is intensified by the subjects he's studying: abnormal psych, psychotic obsession, schizophrenia. As I watch this unfamiliar figure rake a sweaty hand through his too-long gray hair, a new thought chills me: *Is the physician trying to heal himself?*

I can't take it anymore, so I pop back to the theater. When I arrive in the lobby, things are very, very different. It's lighter, brighter on the left side of the stairs. Because the bar's open.

The theater bar was turned into a concession stand a long time ago, but tonight it's back to its 1930s heyday. Shelves of Bombay gin, Johnny Walker, peach schnapps doubled by the mirror behind them. Mahogany bar polished to a dark shimmer. Pinkish lighting under the bottles on the back wall for that let's-go-to-hell-tonight ambiance. Old school barstools in front, all empty.

But the room is not empty. There's a central casting thirties bartender—white shirt, black vest, mustache—behind the bar polishing mugs. Looks to be in his thirties, handsome but a bit worn looking. He doesn't so much as blink when I take a seat in front of him.

"What're ya drinkin'?" he asks in a vaguely Western drawl. Oh man, this is *great*. I'm an old-time movie fan and I feel like I've stepped into a place somewhere between *High Noon* and *Casablanca*.

"I'll take a beer," I say.

He selects a mug and expertly draws me a perfect tap beer. This night is starting to shape up. Drinking and shooting the breeze with some guy out of a classic movie, taking the edge off my weird non-existence for a few hours.

I take a sip of my beer. It's not beer. I don't know what it is—kind of wheaty, neither sweet nor sour—but it's not beer and I tell him so. He doesn't respond; just keeps polishing glasses. So I press him: "I asked you for a beer. Why didn't you give me one?"

"Because you're seventeen," he responds.

Seriously? There's a drinking age in limbo? But I decide not to push any further. The drink's actually not too bad.

"So… why are you here? I mean, tonight, all of a sudden?"

"I work here sometimes." He shrugs, wiping down the bar, though it doesn't need it.

Fair enough. "I'm Hank," I venture.

"I know" is the reply.

Okay. So he knows my name and that I'm seventeen. It dawns on me that this guy is not your garden variety confused specter. For one thing, he doesn't sparkle or fade in and out. He appears solid.

I feel a leap in my chest: maybe this is the guy with the answers.

"So what's the deal with this place?" I ask him. "Why is this the way station for the deceased?"

"Why not?" he replies. "It's a nice place."

Great—the only guy I can talk to isn't giving anything up. But I'm not letting him off the hook.

"It's gotta go deeper than that. What's with all the Egyptian stuff at the top of the stairs?"

"Place of ascension," he says.

"Uh… whatnow?"

"The pyramids," he continues patiently. "They were built as a place of ascension to the afterlife. A stairway to Heaven, if you will."

Stairway to Heaven. *Huh.* I realize this guy knows stuff and suddenly questions start pouring out of me. And not just questions: worries about Margo investigating June's murder. Anger at my brother. Misery about my mom, confusion about Dad. I can see why they say bartenders make the best shrinks: he doesn't give much helpful advice, but at least he listens, and it feels good to get it out.

Finally I ask my Big Question(s):

"Why do I feel the need to stick around? Am I really going to help Margo solve June's murder? Or should I just go up the stairs and leave her alone?"

His answer is "You're here because you need to be."

This annoys me a little and I counter, "Okay, is it a limbo thing, or is there some bartender school where they teach you to make cryptic comments?"

He sets down the mug he's polishing and looks me in the eye for the first time. And here's what he says: "I used to be a miner. It's hard, dark, dirty work, as you might imagine. No one talks in the bucket on the way down. There's a feeling: why bother befriending someone who might not make it out today?"

He leans in, continues: "Every man is isolated in his own space in the tunnel. It's just you, your headlamp, and your pick. Searching, always searching."

He's got me. *Holy crap.* I want to ask what kind of mine he worked in, but I don't want to break the spell of the story.

"It smells somethin' awful down there. And it's cold. But you've got your job and you do it. You search for the sparkle. Just one little sparkle that could turn into a big sparkle and make The Company happy."

He pauses, stares into space, then: "Of course, sometimes very bad things happen down in mines and no one gets out. And the legacy," he jabs a finger here for emphasis, "the *legacy* of that very bad thing goes on and on. It's still happening now. Under the surface."

I wait for more, an explanation of what the hell he's talking about, but the story's over. I can't help but hit him with a reporter's battery of questions: where was this mine? What kind of mine was it? What's the 'legacy'? Is that how you died? In the mine? *Are* you dead, like me?

But he won't answer any of it. I get the feeling he thinks he's already said too much. I try one last question: "Why did you tell me all this?"

Now he looks me in the eye again. "We have a saying down in the mine," he says. "Just keep chipping away."

Just keep chipping away. Fantastic. I've gotten more profound advice from fortune cookies.

He's turned his back to me now. He's done.

But you know what? He's the most interesting guy I've met in a long time, and if 'just keep chipping away' is all he's got for me, I'll take it. Maybe there's something in it.

THIRTY-SEVEN

MARGO

'm skipping school. Not for the whole day, I'll slip in later, but there's something I have to do. I don't think the school secretary will care much anyway; everyone knows my father's sick. Plus I feel about as welcome as the Grim Reaper most places I go. If Margo Pierce doesn't show up for school, no biggie. Less chance of a stray meteor flattening everyone at Lazarus High.

The last thing Dad told Lance was to tail Sam Claypool. That's what Dad thinks Lance is doing. But *I* know that Lance is currently a small boy at a big desk, not tailing anyone, so I've decided it's up to me. It's 8:45 on a Wednesday morning; both Carolyn and Sam should have left for the day by now, so I'm going to pay a little visit to the Claypool house. Uninvited.

Dad was still sleeping when I left. Pre heart attack, he was always up before me, but I guess this is the "new normal"; he's adjusting to his meds and must be exhausted from the stress.

During my usual sleepless stretches last night I was tossing around Dad's theory about Sam. I've decided it's too easy to say this is just the old high school grudge kicking in. But Dad's always had good instincts. Plus I remember the feeling I had at the town council meeting, that Sam wanted Dad dead.

So I've decided to check out Sam's house. I promised Dad I wouldn't go over to June's, but I never said anything about looking around Sam's place. Which is considerably more dangerous since people actually live there. But the good people of Lazarus—and some of the bad—are usually up and off to work at this time, so *here goes.*

As I walk over, head down (nothing to see here, just a high school kid late for school), it occurs to me that it's no accident that I've chosen Wednesday for this mission. It's counselling day. With Boyd. Maybe I can draw this visit out *just* long enough to miss it.

My mind keeps going back to that kiss and I *so wish* I could stop it. *Erase* it. The feeling of Boyd's kiss, the *length* of it.

As Hank kept noting the other night, I didn't immediately pull away, and I'm not sure why. I somehow… wanted the experience, the *connection*. But with Hank or with Boyd? I still don't know.

As for Boyd, it's been radio silence, no texts, no nothing. I'm guessing he's ashamed, and he needn't be. It was just a kiss. It felt nothing like an assault or anything, just a tender reaching out. But if it was "just a kiss," just a blip, why can't I stop thinking about it?

I *have* to stop thinking about it. I'm getting ready to break and enter once again.

I've convinced myself that this *has to be done*, but it's possible that this new felony is just a way of avoiding my late boyfriend's brother. I'm aware that this is nuts, but my feet are walking me to Chestnut Street anyway.

I reach Chestnut, which is actually behind the Claypools' house. As I look at the rock wall at the back of the property, it dawns on me that, in all my sleep-deprived scheming, I never thought about how exactly I'm going to *get inside*. Normally no one locks their doors in Lazarus, but things are different after a murder.

I should really go home.

But quickly—too quickly—I toss reason aside and clamber over the Claypools' wall.

Unsurprisingly, their backyard is *fabulous*. Very impressive, but also somehow rigid in its landscaping. Cypress trees line both sides of the yard, tall, thin, like sentinels watching over the premises. A rectangular swimming pool, empty now. A little square patio shaded by a graceful sycamore, but no leaves on the ground; the gardeners must keep busy making sure Sam Claypool's domain is pristine.

So I'm here. Now, how do I get inside? My mind scrolls through several Mission Impossible–style scenarios: up the drainpipe to the attic window, or drop down through a skylight, remembering to duck infrared sensors.

Then a new thought emerges: if Sam's the murderer, why would he lock his doors? I try the back door to the basement: it swings right open. *Huh.*

I close it behind me, wait and listen for a good five minutes. No sound, not even the cat. I doubt there's much to be learned from the basement rec room so I venture upstairs. If I wasn't here illegally I would stop to admire the interior design: gleaming marble floor in the hall, a granite/walnut super-kitchen, the living room a sage-and-cream wonderland. Not a lot of personality, but they're not exactly artsy types.

I keep moving down the main hallway and quickly find what I'm looking for: Sam's home office. I go in and close the door. It's dark inside, all manly dark wood cabinetry. A computer console. Professional plaques and golf trophies. A framed frozen-smile picture of Sam and Carolyn at some gala.

The danger I've put myself in intensifies my senses and I shift into uber-focus: *I'm here to find June's diary*. If he did kill her and hasn't destroyed it yet, it should be in here somewhere. I have a brief cop-show thought that I should have brought latex gloves, but I didn't so I just plunge in and start digging through every drawer and cabinet. Not much of interest, just lots and lots of paperwork on old and new projects, particularly Willow Grove. Plans, surveys, invoices, contracts... and then something interesting, way in the back of Sam's file cabinet. A report from a soil testing company, for Sam's proposed condo lot. I can't follow all of it, but a few words leap out: "contamination from industrial activity," "inhalation and skin contact concerns," and most of all, "human health risk."

I stop digging and take this in: despite their findings, the soil report deemed Sam's beloved Willow Grove condo project *inhabitable*. But what's even worse is what's stapled to the report: a copy of a check for thirty thousand dollars, made out to the company from Sam.

Either that was one hell of an expensive soil test or Sam paid them off to keep quiet. This is clearly criminal activity; Dad was right about Sam. But could June have found out?

I close my eyes and picture her, daylight glinting off her glasses as she stared, sphinxlike, at the community around her. *June always found out.*

I'm so rattled that I almost miss the very last file in the cabinet. It's as alarming as the soil test, for me, anyhow. It's a file called "JoAnn." A simple manila folder in Sam's file cabinet. I pull it out, my hands starting to shake.

It's mostly old newspaper clippings about my mother. Several stories on her murder. Her obituary. A copy of the police report in my dad's shaky handwriting. The program from her funeral. Plus older clippings about my mom's life: an old Garden Club announcement, a story about her joining the town council. Her wedding announcement. An old swim team picture of her from high school. Mom. A dark-haired beauty queen who didn't act like one.

I feel like I might throw up. *Why does Sam Claypool have comprehensive documentation of my mother's life and death?* I knew he'd competed with my dad for her attentions back in high school, but this looks more like an obsession. The kind of thing police find in a stalker's apartment.

I'm about to put my head between my legs to get my breathing back to normal when I hear someone moving around upstairs. *Time to run.*

I look at the office windows. Would opening them trip an alarm? The sound is still upstairs; maybe I have time to make it out the door. I put the folder back and slip out into the hall. Just in time to hear someone coming downstairs. No time to get out so I dart through the kitchen and slip into a pantry. A tiny room with no exit—*not a good choice.* I look around insanely for coffee—that's what people want first thing in the morning, right? If he or she comes in here for it, I'm screwed. Then I realize I actually smell coffee, and that's why I thought of it. There was a state-of-the-art coffee maker on the kitchen counter making a fresh brew.

Once the coffee crisis is resolved, I give in to curiosity and peek around the corner. There's Carolyn in a white bathrobe. Pretty without makeup, long red hair perfectly tousled, barefoot. Why isn't she at school? Later classes today maybe?

I should have thought of that, should have researched her schedule. My middle-of-the-night ideas often show holes in the daytime.

Carolyn's leaning over the counter now, one bare leg lit by morning sunlight. A weird thought occurs to me: she looks like a magazine ad for ladies' razors. Weirder still is what I realize she's actually doing: petting a hamster. Cooing endearments to it.

This is so not the Carolyn Claypool I've come to know and hate. Standing there cuddling this furry little creature, she actually looks soft, even kind. *Maybe Hank and I have misjudged her,* I think. *Maybe Carolyn-at-home is a sweetie pie.*

So why is my blood running cold?

Chemistry. Scientists and rodents. Lab rats. Maybe I'm just being paranoid—I do live in a town with a high mortality rate—but I have a strong feeling that hamster is not long for this world.

I hold my breath for about an hour, or however long it takes for Carolyn to finally go upstairs, get dressed, and leave the house. Then I'm out the back door, over the wall, and hunched over on Chestnut Street, hyperventilating.

I *did* gather information—about the soil test and the file on my mother—but nothing I can tell Dad. So this is *my* case now, mine to solve, clearly without the requisite skills. My whole body's shaking as I walk to school.

I slip into Mrs. Halverstam's American history class, trying to calm down. But I quickly become obsessed with the classroom clock: 10:40. 10:45. 10:49.

Counseling starts at eleven. There's no skipping it now, and given the morning's events it's clear that I actually *need* some kind of counseling. So I go.

The session starts off pretty quietly: Counselor Mike rattles off whatever information he's supposed to cover this week. Boyd and I look everywhere but at each other. Then Boyd finally gets the nerve to look at me. Stare me down, actually. And finally he does something radical for Boyd-in-Therapy: he speaks. He cuts right through Mike's monologue, talking straight to me.

"Look, I'm really sorry. I was drunk. It won't happen again."

I hesitate, because here's a chance to stand up for women and girls everywhere about unwanted advances, but instead I go with my gut.

"It's okay, Boyd. It was just a kiss. It was nothing."

At this, his jaw sets. He fixes me with his earth-brown eyes and says: "It wasn't nothing to *me*."

I'm taken aback and have to settle my nerves a little before I tell him, maybe a little over-primly: "Well it *has* to be."

Silence as the stare down continues. I notice there's just a touch of amber in the centers of Boyd's eyes. It's mesmerizing.

Mike fills the void by giving us a stern lecture on alcohol abuse and assault, and how he'll have to report this, etc., etc. But I'm tuned out. Because as I stare at Boyd I'm seeing years flash by. Boyd at nine, tanned and sweaty in summertime, tagging along with Hank and me to get ice cream downtown. Silent the whole time as Hank and I one-upped each other with fifth grade humor, just friends then, but already *connected*. Boyd trailing behind as we laughed, giving each other early-mating-dance shoulder punches.

Then Boyd at twelve, coming to the movies with us and receding into the darkness as Hank and I held hands, held each other's knees, locked lips.

Boyd last year at Hank's seventeenth birthday party, scooping ice cream for everyone while I sat on Hank's lap and helped him cut the cake.

Always the outsider to love. Of course he wanted to kiss me.

Mike is waiting for an answer to some question that both of us missed, but that's okay. Boyd and I finally got it out, this thing between us.

Afterward I'm glad I have to hurry off to my next class. I just catch a glimpse of Boyd's maroon-hoodied shoulders disappearing around a corner. So that's that. *Right?*

THIRTY-EIGHT

HANK

ust keep chipping away. You're here because you need to be.
These twin homilies have been swimming around in my head
since last night with the miner/bartender. I have no idea what
to make of his spooky mine disaster story, but the homilies start
to resonate. The remix comes out something like, *I'm here because I need to help Margo keep chipping away at the murder
case.*

So I guess I have a new sense of purpose, which is something a ghost really needs.

I pop over to her house, but she's left for school already. I
look for her at school, but I can't find her. Strange. I can usually
sense where she is.

I'm out in the school parking lot trying to pick up Margo's
location when a familiar red Hyundai drives by me. My mom's.
This is odd. There are no parent-teacher conferences this time of
year, and she's not on any committees.

She parks but doesn't get out so I pop into her car, all the
time thinking, *Please, God, not the pistol in the purse again.* But

she's writing a note. I just manage to get a look at it before she folds it up. It says, "I know what you're up to." *Uh-oh.*

They're not surprised to see her in the school office. And they're so busy that no one notices when she slips the note into Carolyn Claypool's mailbox.

"I know what you're up to." But what is *Mom* up to? My mother, who's so alien to me now. I mentally rewind and land on the time I caught her spying at Carolyn's. My conclusion is, she *doesn't* know *exactly* what Carolyn's up to, but she wants her to know someone's on to her. Does she think she's protecting Sam?

I know they knew each other in high school, may have even dated—not sure. So maybe there's a loopy bravado here.

But I'm not crazy about her next move. On her way out of the school, she runs into Ted Hawkins. He flashes his movie star smile; they had a teasing, flirty relationship when he was my advisor on the paper. But she scowls at him, then snarls: "I know you were there the night my son died."

He stares at her, gobsmacked, his face not knowing what to do with itself.

Oh Mom, I think, *you just couldn't resist, could you? You had to stick it to him.*

And here's where my top candidate for snake-in-the-garden does the last thing I expect: he starts to cry. And shake. Until he's trembling so hard that my mom actually puts an arm around him. He bends over, trying to collect himself.

Mom helps him stand up, then gently steers him through the double doors into a stairwell, away from prying eyes.

"I... I'm *so* sorry," Ted gasps between convulsive sobs. "I... didn't know what to do."

Mom sits him on the steps, one hand on his arm. I look at her: all the rage is gone. There's an almost beatific peace in her eyes now.

"We didn't see him," Ted continues. "Until it was too late..."

And now she's actually hugging him to her chest, *momming* him. I remember the story about her bringing meals over when his mother was dying. She's known him since he was a troubled kid and she was twenty or so. And now that he's confessed, she's amazingly quick to forgive him. To share the horror of that night—which I know she relives every day—with someone who was *there*.

There's something sickening about this, Mom hugging the guy who ran me over. And yet, I realize I've been wanting this. I've been wanting my old advisor to break down sobbing with guilt over my death. Because I *liked* the guy, I looked up to him. I feel like he wanted me to soar out of Lazarus on brains and talent, like he should have but didn't. Like I should have gotten to but didn't.

So I'm in this scene, I'm part of the hug. They just don't know it.

THIRTY-NINE

MARGO

I lay low for the rest of the school week. Try to be who Dad wants me to be: just a high school kid worrying about Geometry and the name of Andrew Jackson's vice president, not murder clues.

I blew off the school paper meeting on Thursday. I just don't have the mental bandwidth to come up with clever ideas for stories when there's only one story I care about.

Dad's become less rebellious and more resigned to bed rest, which actually worries me. I'm afraid of him slipping into the depression Dr. James warned about. Today's Saturday, so I take the time to make him a full breakfast to have in bed: eggs, whole wheat toast, cantaloupe. A small, cheerful sunflower in a vase.

But when I bring him the tray, he looks at it and shakes his head. He doesn't want it. I make him take his pills, but then he just thanks me and rolls over to go back to sleep. *So not Dad.*

I'm back in the living room easy chair fretting when Delia surprises me again at the front door. I open it to find her in a cocky cowgirl pose, complete with overalls, a plaid shirt, and a wisp of straw in her mouth. She's come to drag me to the Fall Harvest Festival. She mentioned it the other day, but I totally forgot.

Hank and I decided when we were around twelve that we were way too cool for all that 4H/hay bale/petting zoo stuff. But my dear Delia is a willful creature when she wants to be and before I know it, we're off for a day of cornball Nebraska wholesomeness.

And here's the shocker: the festival is a *blast*. Just the day itself is breathtaking. Brilliant blue sky over just-harvested cornfields. Little kids skittering around, trying to climb the hay bale pyramid, feeding carrots to cows and goats. Cinnamon deliciousness wafting over from the pie stand. Indian summer warmth on my skin and just a reassuring *home* feeling, bringing me back from my explorations of life's darker side.

Delia and I get candy apples and go to watch the hay bale rolling contest. They do it in the same mini-stadium where the 4H people show their animals. Which is nothing much: a couple of bleachers, a big field, and a crackly loudspeaker system. This is a relay event and the three teams have already assembled at one end near a row of round bales.

The competition allows any age or gender; it's fun to see burly dads lined up alongside high school kids, laughing moms and one ten-ish boy decked out in full cowboy regalia. As we take our seats, we hear the announcement of the teams' self-chosen names: the High Rollers, the Flying Corndogs, and Bailey's Comets. The crowd laughs. I can hear the sound of a bluegrass band skimming the breeze from the other side of the festival. Why did I not want to come to this? Plus it's so good to have Delia by my side. We've both been so *weighed down* for so long; we deserve a break.

The starting pistol goes off and I feel a *good* surge of adrenaline. The first in a long time. I decide I'm for the Flying Corndogs just because they have the best name. Delia and I cheer

them on, waving our apples like red pom-poms against the cloud-
less blue sky.

The three teams of ten are pretty well matched—even the
ten-year-old shoulders his bale down the field with impressive
determination, to huge cheers from the stands. The contest moves
along pretty quickly; we're already down to the last three competitors on each team. Which is when I realize that the guy in the
clean-up spot for the Corndogs is one Boyd James. And he is
ready. I can tell by his wrestler-like stance that he's poised to
spring into action. And confident-looking—if there's one thing
Boyd knows how to do, it's to move an unwieldy object down a
field.

So when it's finally his turn, the surprise isn't that Boyd
toasts the other two competitors, leading the Corndogs to an easy
victory. The surprise is my reaction to watching him do it.

I've watched Boyd play football and never thought much
about it, but there's something about him today in his jeans,
boots, and sleeveless flannel shirt, muscling that bale down the
field that is, well, *stirring*. He's all biceps, sweat, and focus, and
I find myself cheering him on like a madwoman.

I look over at Delia, who's doing the same, and suddenly I
feel guilty. It's okay for her, but not for me. So I lay back a bit as
Boyd heaves his bale over the finish line.

When it's all over but the cheering, Delia makes a beeline
for Boyd, jumping on him by way of congratulations. I drag my
feet a bit, finally catching up with them just as the victorious
Corndogs are getting their picture taken. Boyd lights up when he
sees me; I congratulate him awkwardly. Then we're both mum-
bling conversation about the best way to wheel rolled hay when
Delia breaks in with a challenge: she *swears* she can beat us both
to the top of the hay pyramid. Without even thinking, I shout,
"Hell, I can beat you both!"

And we're off, giddy, the three of us barreling toward the
pyramid, scaring some of the smaller children off. Suddenly I

really want to win. I might not have Boyd's brute strength but
I'm agile and my legs are longer than Delia's, so I have a chance.
I leap on to hay level one, then level two, Boyd right beside me.
Delia has resorted to trying to drag us down by our pant legs,
which makes the whole thing *hilarious*.

Boyd is ahead of me now and I don't like it, though I
couldn't tell you why. So I grab him by the belt loop, hoist myself up, kneel on his shoulder and *throw* myself over the top bale.
He grabs me and then the two of us are tumbling backwards, hitting each level on the way down. When gravity finally flattens
us, there's Boyd next to me, splayed out like a sexy cowboy,
straw in his hair.

He cocks one eyebrow at me and says, deadpan: "I'm afraid
I'm going to have to give you a fifteen-yard penalty for un-
sportsmanlike conduct."

"Oh yeah?" I roll over to face him. "Show me the hay pyramid climbing rulebook."

If he was Hank I'd kiss him right now. But he's *not*.

Delia flops down next to us, noting, "You're both cheaters.
But sort-of congrats, Marg. And clearly there's only one way to
celebrate."

Ten minutes later the three of us are circle-riding ponies that
are way too small for us, annoying the more age-appropriate
children. Laughing our fool heads off. I'm on a sweet little dun
mare who's completely ignoring me, Delia's on a cute little
chestnut named Daisy. But Boyd's the funniest on a little pinto,
his long legs hanging down, hollering, "Go Horsey! Go Horsey!"
until I think I might pee myself.

Goddamn, this is what we needed.

I remember Hank saying once, "Sometimes all you need is a
good time in the middle of a bad time." And this is it: a good
time in the middle of a bad time. And it feels *so good*.

Later on, after listening to the band and scarfing down actual
corndogs and pie, Boyd offers to drive me home. After all, he

lives closer to me than Delia. Delia gives me a look. I'm about to say, *No, I came with Delia.* But I don't. "Sure," I say.

And then there we are, the two of us in Hank's old car (which Boyd drives now), driving home as the sun sinks low in the sky. And I *cannot* think of a word to say. Boyd is usually quiet, so it's up to me to fill in the gaps, but all I can come up with is "That apple pie was *amazing*, wasn't it?" to which he agrees. Then more silence. Compounding the situation is an old friend of mine, a purple lizard that I won for Hank in a claw machine. We named him Leonard, and he's still crouched on the dashboard where Hank left him. I swear he's looking at me. Judging me.

Boyd flips the radio on and boy is it the wrong song: Ed Sheeran's "Thinking Out Loud."

Baby I will be lovin' you till we're seventy...

Beautiful song; totally tenses us both up. Me, because of what's coming: *He's going to kiss me again.* Right? The day seems to call for it. But the worst thing is, in my heart of hearts, do I actually want him to? Because if Hank's watching—and he probably is—that's it, game over. He'll be up those stairs to the afterlife before you can say Omaha.

Boyd pulls up in front of my house, stops. I look at him; there's that spark of amber in his eyes again. But all he does is say, "Great day," to which I over-nod. Is he just being respectful? Either way, the day, date, whatever it was, is over. I thank him for the ride and then hop out.

Watch him pull away in my late boyfriend's car. Same car, new driver. It's all *very* confusing.

FORTY

HANK

Of course I was watching. And now I want to throw up. It really, really looks like my girlfriend has moved on. With my brother. I want to die, and I'm already dead.

I start walking around the now-dark town. Maybe on the way back to the theater, maybe to finally go up those steps, I don't know. Just walking.

As I step on to Main Street I see a familiar car pass by: Dan McNamara's. Windows partway down; I can hear his awful music again. But for some reason, I hop in with the guy. Let's go sling some dope, howl at the moon. He doesn't even creep me out anymore. I feel like we're two lost soulmates. But as we ride out of town I realize that I'm not just here out of kinship with another troubled dude. I want to solve the mystery, finish the job so I can *move on*. I'm ready.

Somewhere near Norfolk, Dan pulls us into a very unsavory-looking abandoned warehouse type area. Perfect for illicit hand-offs. We go deeper into this corrugated maze until we're in a completely dark area, save for Dan's headlights. And then he shuts them off and I feel like I'm reliving my death, it's so dark. A door opens; a vertical rectangle of light with red-painted walls inside. There's a guy in the doorway, waiting. Okay, this is getting interesting now. Margo and Boyd can have their hokey day at the fair. I'm in a particularly suspenseful episode of *Cops*.

The guy in the doorway says one word: "Yo." Which Dan repeats. I follow them both in.

Whatever this place is, it could use an HGTV makeover: patches of odd paint colors, rusted metal, all lighting from single bulbs hanging from the ceiling. Whatever's done in this building, I doubt it's very wholesome. I take a deep breath and keep following. Up clangy metal stairs, down another hall with no light at all. But a partly open door at the end of the hall provides enough light to find our way. When we get there, the Yo guy opens the door.

To say that what's inside is unexpected is an understatement. On the walls, on a console, filling the whole room, really, is a shit ton of *recording equipment*. How Dan fits into this is utterly beyond me.

"You want to review or start the third track?" the Yo guy asks Dan.

"Start three," Dan answers. Both of them put headphones on. Dan gets out a notebook, flips to a page with writing on it. Yo flips a switch; a beat starts up. Then, at Yo's signal, Dan starts *rapping*. Rapping loudly, rapping badly, with Yo recording the whole thing.

I have to sit down on a nearby amp.

Dan McNamara's not a drug dealer. He's a *would-be rapper. Very* would-be, 'cause it *ain't gonna happen, brother.* The lyrics I can make out are mostly lame, but after a few minutes, I stop judging. Whatever this guy's demons are, he's found a way to get them out. If I had a job trimming the gristle off meat all day, I might yell bad poetry for a hobby too.

I've stopped judging, but I can't actually sit and listen to the stuff anymore. And I'm pondering: If Danny Mac's not a pot dealer, what's Mrs. Mac doing with those plants?

I pop back to her house. It's a pleasant scene after the recording-studio-from-hell: antique lamps lit, a ginger cat curled up on a purple afghan on the couch. Tony Bennett singing from an old radio; now *that's* the kind of retro stuff I can get behind.

And Mrs. Mac herself, in a well-worn beige sweater, sitting at the dining room table bagging pot.

FORTY-ONE

MARGO

After I watch Boyd pull Hank's car away, I'm more confused than ever. So it's with a feeling of guilty excitement that I meet the scene inside.

My dad's slumped on the couch watching some stupid game show. Dad never watches TV, except for sports or news once in a while. But here he is, staring vacantly at some extremely lame show where contestants swim though foam and get bonked by large rubber objects. He doesn't even look up when I come in. "Hey Dad," I venture, and he finally turns to me.

I've never seen this look in his eyes before: so lost, so sad. Like he's given up. I don't really know the signs of clinical depression, but this sure looks like it and it scares me.

"How was school?" he asks. I tell him it's Saturday; he just nods. I ask him if he wants some dinner but he doesn't respond.

I'm still so jittery from the day I've had, I feel like I might cry. But I don't. I go into the kitchen and heat up some heart-healthy Chinese food Zhen has made us. When it's ready, I turn off the TV and gently lead my father to the table. He stares at his steaming chicken and string beans for a moment, then pokes it with his fork.

This is bad. I don't like this. Is this depression or is he over-medicated? I have to talk to Dr. James about this.

At a loss for conversation, I ask him how his day was. He thinks for a minute, then says: "Hank was here. We were horsing around. Wrestling."

I put down my fork. "Hank was here?"

"Yeah," he responds, then starts eating. I don't bother to correct him.

I remember Hank telling me that he "wrestled" Dad back into his body when he was dying. Is it possible that in his current drugged state he remembers that? Or does this mean he's dying again?

I can't eat another bite. I excuse myself and go call Dr. James, my phone hand trembling. When I tell him what's going on, he says it's to be expected: a slump after returning from the hospital. Plus his body's still adjusting to the new meds. Just ride it out and be there for him, he says. It'll get better.

When I return to the table, Dad has nodded off. This is so nursing home; unbearable. I can't get him upstairs, but I prod him awake and lead him back to the couch, where he immediately falls back asleep. Staring at him asleep on the couch, I finally let the tears flow. Something in his posture tells me he's given up and that's unbearable to me. Not Dad. I can't take it, I really can't. We've survived all these losses *together*, but now it feels like he's leaving me.

Who are you in this world if you lose everyone you love? And who loves you? What do you become? Just a dried-out husk, and not the cute ones people put on their doors in the fall. Just scarred and empty.

The doorbell rings; I do not want to answer it. *What fresh hell could this be?*

But I'm glad I do because there, under the porch light, is Delia, now changed into her more Delia-ish checked jacket and black beret. At first I think she's pissed about Boyd driving me home, but then I see it's something else. She hesitates for a minute, then says:

"I know you've been trying to solve June's murder because I know you. We spent the whole day together and you didn't mention it once. What is *up?*"

I immediately defensively note that it was a *fall festival* and we were riding *ponies*. Why would I bring that up?

"Why do you think I made you go?!" Delia bleats. "You've been the world's most serious, closed-up teen detective since June died. You *gotta* let me in, kid," she insists. "Marg and Deel, *always*. Remember?"

This gets me; *boy* does it get me. *Delia*. I *haven't* lost everyone.

And suddenly we're hugging and laughing and crying as moths dance in the porch light over our heads.

We go up to my room and I tell her everything I've been keeping from her: Lance, Gib, Ted, Carolyn and the hamster, even Boyd. It feels *so good* sharing it all with Delia. By the time I'm done, we're two sixteen-year-olds again, instead of two people staggering under burdens too heavy to bear alone.

Delia's eyes start to sparkle as she considers every suspect, and I realize, *Crap, here's my Watson*. Every Sherlock needs a Watson.

It feels so good that I come *this close* to telling her about Hank. But I don't. Because as good as it feels to share the load, me and Hank can only be me and Hank. That's just how it is.

FORTY-TWO

HANK

'm back at the theater, reliving the Fall Festival Hallmark romance. I can't stop thinking about it.

The thing is, even I would put Margo and Boyd together. They're both great looking, with dark hair, dreamy brown eyes. Kinda like one of those perfect pictures that comes with a store-bought frame. Who am I in this scenario—who was I ever—but the comic relief?

And what a story it would be. The kind of story reality TV producers seize on: beautiful girl loses her boyfriend in a tragic accident, then finds love again with his handsome, grieving brother. Together, they overcome the sad past and find joy again. *Perfect.*

These are my self-pity-soaked thoughts as I skulk around the Egyptian. I've been playing the alto sax for two days straight now, and I still can't shake the gloom. Finally I put the sax down and lie down on the floor, looking up at the starry night sky ceiling mural. There's the Big Dipper. Orion. Did the ancient Egyptians do astronomy? Or do the gold stars against midnight blue paint just look good? So many holes in my education that will never be filled.

And then I think, sadly: I'm *done*. I can't be a jealous ghost drifting around purgatory anymore. It's too pathetic.

Someone needs to help Margo solve this crime, but it's not me. And honestly, I don't want it to be Boyd. So... *who?* Suddenly it occurs to me: if the police chief isn't up to this job, his *deputy* needs to step up. Yes, Lance Ritter is a hapless boob who just got thrown under the Life Crisis bus, but you know what? There's a lot of that going around. So I stand up, pop over to Lance's place, and sit on his bed until he wakes up. Weird, yes, but the guy's been AWOL and someone needs to keep tabs on him.

Lance wakes up with a shudder; his eyes pop open like a frightened baby's. Then he steadies himself, and as he gets up and completes his morning routine, I see something unfamiliar in him: *determination*. Even brushing his teeth, Lance suddenly has the locked-down visage of a seasoned Marine. I've never met this Lance, and I'm intrigued.

Out in the living room there's a major change. All the superhero posters are gone. Looking around, I don't see so much as a Wolverine mug. Instead of the posters on the long interior wall is an enormous zoning map of Lazarus. Each lot, each house, each commercial and public building in town. And many, many handwritten notes coded in red, blue and green ink. Acronyms like HWF, BTS, and NA, plus circles, pushpins, and stars for emphasis. I try to read the notes, but Lance's handwriting is a wild scribble.

As I lean in, I can make out that each house bears the name of the family who lives there. Several houses are marked with a single word in red: *gun*.

As I assess this spectacle, I wonder: am I witnessing the emergence of an actual detective? Or something more sinister. Is Lance *protecting* the homes pictured here? Or targeting them?

Lance leaves out the kitchen door, descends the back stairs, gets in his car—a Honda, not the squad car—and drives out of town. I'm the unseen ride-along in the passenger seat. On the outskirts of Norfolk, he pulls into a strip mall. Grabs a gym bag and heads into a little gym. Nothing fancy, just one of those sweaty-mat-and-fluorescent-lights bodybuilding gyms, sparsely populated on a weekday.

And as I watch him work out, *that's* what bugs me. It's Monday, a *workday*. While my girlfriend is busting her ass trying to solve his colleague's murder (*and* get her high school homework done) the deputy is at the gym pumping iron.

After the workout, our next stop—also in the strip mall—is less annoying, more compelling. Lance goes to a firing range. And here's the surprise: he's a pretty good shot. He must have been practicing. Our Lance appears to be on a self-improvement kick.

But it's more than that: as I watch him fire off round after round, fiercely focused, I think of the contrast between this guy and the man-child I saw bawling on the floor of his apartment. Has the death of his mother finally jolted Lance into maturity? And professional responsibility? Or has this proficient gunman always been in there, behind the innocent mask?

FORTY-THREE

MARGO

IT guys are so weird. When I called to check on the status of June's hard drive, the guy didn't even respond, he just put down the phone for ten minutes while he and some other genius looked for it. When he finally got back to me, all he said was, "Yeah, we're pretty backed up." So I'm not expecting much from Cyber Salvage.

I finally got Dad's permission to pack up June's house, but I don't feel good about it. I brought him breakfast in bed again this morning and insisted he take a few bites. As he munched grumpily on toast I re-floated the idea: I could do it after school today. He really just grunted in reply. Not permission exactly. But he didn't shut me down either. He couldn't.

So it's with this feeble authorization that I now carry packing boxes and tape up June's front walk. I'll scour the house for clues, then pack up her possessions, separating out some things I think Lance might want. The rest will go to Goodwill.

I thought about asking Delia to help me, now that she's in the loop, but I didn't. June's house is too sacred to me now. I need to do this alone.

As I turn the key and push open the door, I realize I'm holding my breath. Here it is, just as June left it. No forensics team has upturned it for clues; I'm the first one to open this door since the murder. The weight of being the town's entire detective squad suddenly feels very heavy.

The house is a one-story bungalow: just a living room, kitchen, bath, bedroom, and a tiny second bedroom. I've been here many times before—June used to babysit me—and the familiarity chokes me up. All the June-ish things: the old couch she called a "davenport," her TV trays where she'd set up dinner for us in front of *Judge Judy*. Man, we had fun ragging on the *Judge Judy* defendants. A framed picture of Jesus praying, his heart beaming yellow from under his white robe. Hank's been over here too, and we always giggled about the picture's over-the-topness. We called it Glowheart Jesus. But today it's kind of how I feel: like my heart's coming out of my chest.

One thing I ponder now is June's love of all things Mexican. The vibrant red, mustard yellow, and white serape draped over the couch, a hammered tin cross on the wall, Guadalajara cactus salt and pepper shakers in the kitchen. A collection of Day of the Dead figures—skeletons playing instruments, getting married, picnicking. That seems ominous now. I used to play with them when I was too young to know they were creepy.

I have to wonder where she got all this stuff. You don't see a lot of it for sale around here. Online maybe, but I don't think so. These items seem more like cherished souvenirs. Did she take trips to Mexico? Why Mexico? For I second I shift into paranoid overdrive: *Mexico, drugs, cartels, payback, execution.* And then I immediately feel guilty. Anyone I know who's been to Mexico found a beautiful country, rich in culture and kind people. Why *wouldn't* June be attracted to it?

And the idea that June was gunned down by a vengeful Mexican drug lord is ludicrous. She probably just picked these things up in Lincoln. There are some artsy ethnic shops over there.

Anyhow, what I'm really looking for is "Chesapeake." Anything about Maryland or Virginia. Is that where she was from? It's ridiculous that I know so little about a woman that was practically my aunt.

As I head for the kitchen, a photo on the wall makes me catch my breath. It's a picture of my family—me, my mom and dad—with June. We have our arms around each other, smiling, the sun in our eyes.

Mom, radiating earthy beauty: laughing brown eyes, thick dark hair, brilliant smile. She glows with life in every picture, which feels like a sucker punch. Her arm's around me: a natural, casual, motherly thing that just slays me now. I have to steady my breath, try to examine the picture clinically.

I look like I'm about six or seven; I'm making a silly face for the camera. And Dad: such a different, younger look on his face. Before the weight pressed down on his shoulders. It's all just sunny and happy and innocent. *Before.*

June's smile is a bit tamer than ours, a bit shy. Maybe she feels like she's infringing on our family. We *were* her family, I realize. This is the only photo she has up in the house.

I exhale and head into the kitchen. Not much in there: red vinyl diner chairs at a small table. Grocery list on the fridge. The Guadalajara shakers.

I go into June's bedroom. The late afternoon sun slanting in on June's tidily made bed gives me another lump in my throat. *She'll never sleep here again.* Don't be melodramatic, I tell myself, but it doesn't work. It's all so *final.* So sad.

I open her closet and look through her clothes. Mostly sensible skirts, slacks, and blouses. I linger at her Christmas sweater, tracing my finger over the green sequined tree. So familiar it hurts. The only thing that stands out in her generally subdued wardrobe is yet another Mexican item: a white and red peasant blouse with gold trim paired with a black and gold flared skirt. I puzzle over the outfit. It's like June had this secret, flamboyant life in Mexico.

I move on to an antique walnut desk under a picture window on the back wall. I'm holding out a faint hope that I might find her diary, but I doubt it. It was always at the office.

The first drawer is disappointing—just office supplies—but the second answers the big question of the afternoon. Inside is a photo envelope filled with pictures of a Mexican vacation. Young June with longer hair on a romantic trip with a slightly older man. As I peer at the man's ruggedly handsome face— strong jaw, piercing eyes—I realize it's Gib. Young Gib was actually kinda hot, which is shocking considering the craggy preacher of today. I guess Ted had to get it from somewhere.

But the real surprise is the scope of their affair. This was not just a fling; these two *vacationed* together. Were happy together.

The last picture is the most informative. It's just June, seated, looking up at the camera. She's wearing the outfit in the closet. The white of the blouse sets off a deep tan. Her legs are coyly crossed, her neckline pulled low—she looks straight up sexy. But the real information comes from her face: more open than I've ever seen, filled with warmth and light. No hard lines around her mouth yet. Gazing up at the photographer with pure adoration. As I stare at it, I realize without a doubt June didn't just date Gib. She was in love with him.

Which leads to new questions: What became of Ted's mom? The hospital bed Hank saw suggests a long illness, but when and how did June come into the picture? And why didn't June and Gib get together after her death?

There's one last room to check. My expectations are so low for the little laundry room by the back door that I almost miss it: a tiny flash of color behind the dryer.

I lean over and reach until I grab something: a large white poster board. I pull it out.

There are a million little notes on it, a timeline, Post-its, names of various people in town plus comments about them.

But it's the title at the top of the board that makes me gasp: *JoAnn.*

FORTY-FOUR

HANK

So Lance is off superheroes, working out, and becoming a crack shot. This news is interesting enough to present to Margo, but I don't. I'm still not ready to be her plucky detective partner while she swoons around with my brother. So I go looking for the bartender instead. Maybe he'll have some insight into Lance 2.0.

But the bar's closed. All's quiet in ancient Egypt today.

I'm just about to suck it up and visit Margo when I see something glowing in the darkness below the staircase. It's a spirit—very faint—but I can tell it's a woman.

I cross to her slowly; new spirits startle easily. She starts to come into focus: a pale, sickly looking woman in a dressing gown. I welcome her and ask her if she's just passed.

"No," she says, "I passed quite a while ago. I was ill." I can see this on her face: raw, red-blotched skin, patchy hair. *Chemo.*

I nod, wait for more. She tells me she's been in After and can't imagine why she's been brought back here.

"So you were here before?" I ask her. "At this way station? Did you live around here?"

"I lived on a farm," the woman noted. "On the old Graham Road."

Bing, bing, bing. Gib's farm's on the old Graham Road.

"Were you married to Gib Hawkins?" I ask gingerly, afraid she'll disappear before I can get all my questions out.

"Yes," she says, but then her face darkens. Then glitters more brightly, with righteous anger. "I was true to my vows," she asserts. "*I* was true."

"And he wasn't?" I follow up. "Did he break his marriage vows? With a woman named June?"

Now the spirit flares into dark, iridescent colors, blues and purples swirling with pained emotion.

"What do you know about it?" she grills me. "Who are you?"

"Hank James," I tell her. "I passed this summer. I just want to find out…"

"I was at peace, finally, in After. And then *she* arrived. My nurse. She was hired to be my nurse. She came into our home. And then she and my husband…" She flicks her hand disgustedly.

So June used to be a nurse. How did we not know that? She must've buried that part of her life. *I tried to live a good life after. Tried to make it right.*

"June Hudspeth," I say, and Mrs. Hawkins just looks away, pained. *Wow*, I think. Knowing June and Gib as senior citizens, it's hard to picture the torrid affair that crushed a dying woman's soul. But I can see it on her spirit's face.

"Did June… send you back?"

"No!" she scoffs. Then more softly: "I came to check on my boy."

It takes me a second to realize she means Ted.

"How is he?" she asks tentatively.

"He's fine," I lie. "Teaches English at the high school."

I think about helpfully noting that she could probably watch him on video in the theater, but think better of it. *Don't try to be the perfect concierge, just keep chipping away.*

"Mrs. Hawkins," I say. "I'm trying to find out how June died. She was murdered…"

But she's not listening.

"My boy was so sweet," she murmurs. "So handsome. In my last weeks, he would lie with me. Brush my hair, hold my hand."

I feel a pang of sympathy for young Ted. That's incredibly tough stuff for a kid.

Now Gib's wife starts to falter, tears in her eyes. "He didn't want me to *see*. My husband with her. *That's* why he did it."

Why he did it. A tingle goes up my spine.

"What did Ted do?" I ask her gently.

"He used a pillow. He was always strong."

Sonovabitch. Ted smothered his mom.

"I struggled," she continues. "But not for long. I wanted it. He *knew* I wanted it."

Holy crap, I think. Ted euthanized his dying mother to save her from both physical and emotional agony. That is *horribly* amazing. And in a weird way, an ultimate act of love.

Now Mrs. Hawkins starts to sob, arms fluttering. "I want to go *back!* Can you help me go back?"

"Yes," I say, though I'm not really sure. "Just go up the stairs." I can't grill this wretched soul anymore.

She looks up the stairs, uncertain. I reach for her arm and am able to grasp it. I walk her to the front of the staircase. Then wonder: will I have to walk her all the way up? And if I do, will I get whooshed away too? And is that maybe what I really want?

No, I realize. *I want to stay here and help Margo.*

But Mrs. Hawkins steps up herself. Starts walking up the stairs.

When the music begins, it's different. Not a triumphal chorus, just soft and pleasant, like summer wind through pines. The light isn't as bright as usual either. The mural still sparkles, but it's more like a moonlit night in antiquity. When Gib's wife is finally swept away, it's gentle, like she's being welcomed back.

As the light in the theater returns to normal, I wonder: Was she somehow brought back to talk to me? To tell me that she was Gib's wife and Ted's mother? And that Ted smothered her?

I shiver and realize it's not because I'm cold. It's because I'm getting that feeling again: *Someone in town's going to die soon.*

FORTY-FIVE

HANK

This would be fun if it wasn't about my mom's murder. Delia and I are sitting on my bed, studying the whiteboard like we're working on a project for school. My Lady Gaga poster stares down at us from the wall above, cans of pomegranate seltzer are on hand, the scene's lit by my thrift store llama head lamp—funky teendom plus murder investigation.

I always knew June was trying to solve my mom's case. Not that she talked to me about it; she wouldn't do that. But she and Mom were close, and June was a detective at heart. She needed to know what was going on in her town, and this unsolved puzzle must have driven her crazy.

Some of her notes are obvious—I've thought of them myself—but others are surprising.

Sam Claypool carried a torch for her. Did she rebuff him?

I know this one. This theory has lived in my house for seven years—my dad's obsessed with it. But Sam had a solid alibi: he was at a bowling tournament the night my mother was killed. Dad interviewed every last bowler and Lazarus Lanes employee:

could Sam have slipped out at some point? But by all accounts, Sam was front and center all night, trying to bring home the trophy for his team.

There's one word on the board for Carolyn Claypool: *jealous?*

I get what she's suggesting, but I don't see it. Carolyn strikes me as satisfied to have a meal ticket relationship with her husband. It's hard to imagine her flying into a murderous rage over his wandering affections. And God knows *hers* have wandered quite a bit.

The entry for Ted Hawkins is strange: *always flirted with her at the pool.*

That's hardly a headline; who *doesn't* Ted Hawkins flirt with? But I do remember him parking his manly physique next to Mom at the town pool while Dad and I splashed around. Mom humoring him from behind her big brown sunglasses when I'm sure she really wanted to get back to her book.

"Marg—what does this mean?" Delia's pointing to the entry for Gib Hawkins, which reads: *pretty girl at the house.*

"Who's the pretty girl?" she asks.

A memory stirs. "My mom," I finally answer. "I think she brought meals over when Gib's wife was dying. Everyone did."

"And June was around, right? Maybe she saw how he looked at her."

"Everyone looked at her like that" is all I have to offer.

But something about this bothers me. *Pretty girl at the house.* I imagine my mom, who would have been in her early twenties at the time, coming over with a casserole. Offering help, sympathy. Innocent and vulnerable.

"I'm almost offended that *we're* not suspects," Delia jokes, pointing to the Changs' alibi: *running their restaurant.* "Sorry," she adds. "Just trying to lighten the mood. Stupid."

I wave off her apology, re-focusing. The next note shocks me: *Emmie James—did she want Roy?*

What? Fun, wise-cracking Emmie James, happily married to the town doctor, secretly lusting for my father? They did go to high school together. But no, I'm not buying it. Has to be just a random hypothesis.

But there's another note under Emmie's name that's even more chilling: *someone she trusted.*

I sit back. The popular theory on my mom's death is that she accepted a ride from someone she knew, who then killed her and dropped her body off on Route 57.

But Emmie James? I *know* her. I flash on the image of Emmie's eyes on Back-to-School Night, first blank then murderous at the sight of Carolyn. Do I *really* know her?

"Did you see this one?" Delia asks. She's pointing to the entry for Dr. James: *says his whole family died in a fire— convenient. What is he hiding? Did he assume a new identity? Did JoAnn find out?*

"That's crazy" is my first reaction. "Dr. James? A fugitive with a secret past?"

But Delia's not listening. She's got something.

"He wasn't there," she says flatly.

"What?"

Now she fixes me with laser certainty. "Dr. James wasn't at Back-to-School Night. And he *always* comes."

As she continues, I can almost hear the sound of puzzle pieces locking into place. I suddenly have a chilling thought. Has Dr. James been over-drugging Dad so he couldn't work on the case?

"What better time to commit a murder than when you know everyone in town will be somewhere?" Delia concludes.

It's an awful thought. I go into the bathroom to splash water on my face.

"How could you *possibly* think my dad killed June?"

I look up, see Hank's reflection in the bathroom mirror.

"How long have you been watching us?" I ask him.

"Long enough."

I turn to face him.

"So where was he that night?"

At this, Hank hesitates for a second. Then: "Home. I popped in. He was taking a shower."

"Taking a shower," I repeat. Hank knows what I mean. *Maybe he needed to clean up.*

"Hank," I continue. "What do you really know about your dad's past?"

He doesn't answer. Which is an answer.

FORTY-SIX

HANK

Here's what I know about my dad's past: he grew up in a family of five in West Texas. Mom, Dad, sister, brother. One night when he was staying over at a friend's house, the family home burned down with everyone but Dad in it. Cause unknown, though Dad's father was a smoker.

Dad went to live with relatives, finished school, then went north to Chicago for college and medical school. And that's the complete biography.

So yes, there is a blank space where my dad's relatives should be. We've never met so much as a cousin. And for some reason, I've never asked him about them. The family mythology is that Dad's a strong guy who rebounded from a trauma, but we don't talk about that trauma or anything surrounding it. We just let it lie.

And honestly, I don't like having that mythology questioned. I like it. My dad, the poor orphaned kid who grew up to save lives. And I certainly don't want it replaced with Dad-as-fugitive/murderer.

So I'm conflicted and pissed as I accompany Margo on her Girl Detective errands today after school. She strides along; I'm trying to keep up. Stop One: interrogating my father.

"You realize that you're accusing a *doctor*," I grouse at her. "The *healer* who's keeping your father alive."

"I'm not accusing anyone," Margo retorts. "I just want to ask him some questions."

We turn on to my street. So weird. How many times have we done this? Walked from her house to mine? My mom might've been gardening as we approached, Dad mowing the lawn, offering a cheerful wave. *Hundreds* of times. The only difference today is that I'm dead and Margo's interrogating Dad for murder.

I do not believe my father murdered June. So why is Doubt is clomping around my brain in combat boots?

I remember June saying: "I felt bad for both of them." Did she mean my parents, who had just lost a son? Did she find something out about my dad, and give him the courtesy of a heads up before she told Roy? And he shot her?

No. It's too much, too cop show. I *refuse* to believe it.

We're there; Margo rings the doorbell. *Don't be home, don't be home.* He's home. He opens the door and smiles, surprised but glad to see her.

Margo didn't call ahead. She says her dad says it's better to just show up and read the look on people's faces. The look on Dad's face is both sad and kind, as it's been ever since I died. He invites her in, asks how Roy is doing, offers her iced tea, which she declines.

They sit. Looking around this familiar space—bookshelves over-stuffed with my mom's varied interests, the overhead light chipped from indoor hockey—I kinda hate her. She shouldn't be bringing her detective act into this sacred space where I wrestled my brother and cheered the Twins on with my father.

Dad asks what's on her mind; Margo takes a breath.

"As you know, I've been filling in for my father while he's recovering," she ventures, too formally. "Looking into June Hudspeth's murder."

"Yes," Dad replies patiently. Of course he knows she's been doing that. He knows Margo.

"She was your patient, wasn't she?"

She reminds me of a little girl trying to act older at a pretend tea party as an adult indulges her. Knock it off, Margo.

Dad plays along: "Yes."

"Did she ever discuss anything with you that seemed, I don't know, out of the ordinary?"

"No," my father says softly. And leaves it at that.

Margo continues: "Okay, just one more thing: June died on the night of Back-to-School- Night. Everyone was at the school. Except you, and you always go. Why'd you skip it this year?"

I'm watching my Dad's face. There's the tiniest muscle spasm now on the right side of his forehead. Just a little twitch. And no answer.

Drop in on people and read their faces. Crap.

And suddenly I'm not angry at Margo anymore. I'm *worried* for her, and I hate myself for it.

It suddenly occurs to me how strong my dad is. Athletic. He could kill her with his bare hands if he wanted to.

Why am I thinking that?!

Because of the expression on his face. He's angry and trying to control it.

"Margo," he says finally. "Am I being *interrogated*?"

Margo's crumbling now, trying to maintain composure.

"I just…" she falters. "I just thought it was odd…"

Dad takes a deep breath, hangs his head. Caught? I wish I could grab Margo and bolt out of there.

But when he looks up again, Dad's back. He reaches forward, takes her hands. Margo's still tense, not sure if this is good or bad.

"Margo," Dad continues. "You don't always have to be the good kid. The *responsible* one. Since Hank died, I can barely *walk*. Barely get through my days. You're only sixteen years old. You don't have to be the police chief. Your dad will recover and solve this case."

Now it's Margo's face that's contorting, fighting back tears.

"But... *Thanksgiving*," she rambles. "They said they'll replace him if he doesn't solve the case by Thanksgiving."

"Screw that," says Dad. "No one's replacing Roy Pierce. Screw Sam Claypool and his henchmen."

Margo loses her fight, raining tears now, clutching Dad's hands. So glad he sees through her.

They talk for a little while longer, mostly Dad reassuring her. When she gets up to leave, he hugs her.

I'm fifty pounds lighter as we leave the house. Out in the fall air, so relieved...

...until Boyd appears. Takes Margo's arm.

"I need to talk to you," he insists.

Margo looks at me; I'm too shocked to respond.

She lets Boyd escort her to the backyard for a private conference. Private, except I'm following. They stop between my mother's abandoned, bedraggled garden beds, which seems right.

I'm hoping he's got something useful to tell her about the case. But when he turns to face her, I know it's not that. I'm reading faces again and Boyd's says: *I want you.*

I'm choked by anger and pain. My brother's going to make a play for my girlfriend and there's not a thing I can do about it.

"The other day, the fall festival..." he stutters. "There's something between us, Margo. I know you feel it too."

Margo doesn't respond. She can't. I'm here.

Boyd makes his case by kissing her. Not the drunken snog of the other night but a real, manly, passionate Hollywood kiss. If he wasn't kissing my girlfriend, I'd be impressed.

Margo's clearly impressed because *again*, she doesn't immediately stop him. And the strange thing is, *I get it*. She's a mess and here's her savior, a smitten hunk who could carry her away from all this. Boyd could love her back to happiness and I could go up the stairs. *Done*.

But Margo breaks away, tells him *no*.

"Hank's *gone*," Boyd pleads. "It's *us* now."

Traitor. But he's not wrong. He gently brushes her hair out of her face, which enrages me further: that's *my* move!

"I *can't*," cries Margo.

Boyd's exasperated, trembling. "Why not?" he begs.

"Because he's *not* gone!" Margo yells. "Hank's still here!"

She turns, fumbles with the gate and flees, leaving Boyd devastated. The wounded Minotaur.

Good.

FORTY-SEVEN

MARGO

cannot think about this. I can't feel all this. I've got *work* to do. I shut down that part of my mind—a trick I learned after my mother died—and head over to Mrs. McNamara's house. Because that's what a pro would do, and I have to be a pro now.

I find her in her garden, watering plants, which fits well with the story I've concocted. Mrs. Mac looks so sweet in her powder blue jacket, watering her purple-pink ornamental kale (I've studied up on autumn gardening). She reminds me of one of the illustrations in books my mother used to read me by Beatrix Potter. Mrs. Bunny, tending her garden. It's hard to imagine the scene Hank described the other night: Mrs. Bunny bagging a controlled substance.

She spots me and seems pleased I've stopped by; she turns off the hose to chat. After the opening small talk, which always involves asking after my father these days, I tell her that I'm doing a gardening story for the school paper. I feel guilty at the excitement this incites in her; she immediately starts telling me what a *marvelous* time fall is in the Midwestern garden. She shows me her pink asters, her lavender Russian sage, her russet-colored sedum; I take notes. It really is a stunning garden.

She takes me inside to show me her indoor plants: more leafy gems. As we walk through the living room, I notice something Hank missed, on a side table. It's a framed photo of the Lazarus Garden Club from 2011. There are nine women smiling out from the photo, including the recently deceased June Hudspeth.

So they did know each other. And from their beaming expressions this looks like it was a close-knit group. Close enough to have nicknames for each other.

Could June have known about the pot plants, which was why she planned to "talk to Mac"? Of course she could have. June always knew everything that was going on in town.

My detective resolve returns. I ask to see the greenhouse.

Mrs. Mac's expression doesn't change, but she hesitates. Blinks. Then launches into a rambling excuse why I can't see it:

"Oh it's a mess, I really need to get after it... broken window," she says, then throwing in randomly: "Raccoon."

It's time to come clean. We're facing each other across her dining room table, which wears a lacy white tablecloth from another era. How can I say what I'm going to say? But I have to.

"Mrs. McNamara," I begin. "I've heard that you've been growing pot plants. Marijuana," I add, for emphasis.

Now she blinks twice, saying faintly, "Who on earth told you that?"

"A friend of mine *saw* them. In your greenhouse."

Now the look in her eyes shifts. To something harder. "This isn't really for a gardening story at all, is it?"

"No," I say, realizing that I've done it again. I've accused someone of something in their own home, where they know every cabinet, every drawer that might hold a firearm. Without breaking eye contact, I take a quick mental inventory of every exit available to me.

"Did you know my husband?" she asks me, surprising me.

"Not really," I say. "I know he passed a couple of years ago."

"Two and a half years ago. Liver cancer. And he didn't drink or smoke. One of nature's cruel tricks," she says with a sad smile.

She sits down in one of the chairs, suddenly exhausted by the thought of her husband's death.

"All that chemo, all that suffering, for *nothing*," she says, anger creeping into her voice now. I take the seat across from her. It seems like the thing to do as she delves into this melancholy, intimate topic.

"And all the time I kept thinking: What can I do? How can I help him?" She looks at me directly, her watery blue eyes suddenly fierce. "So I grew marijuana. And it *helped* him. It softened the pain."

I nod. Of *course*. I get it. But we're not done yet. I proceed carefully.

"I *totally* understand that, Mrs. McNamara," I tell her earnestly. "But the thing is, you're still growing it, two years after your husband's death. Growing it, drying it, and bagging it for… sale?" This last word comes out as faint question.

Mrs. McNamara stares at me, all the sweet melancholy gone. Her eyes are devoid of emotion. They're almost clinical, appraising me.

"Would you like to see them?" she finally asks me. The sweetness is back, but it's an affectation, a put-on.

"The plants?" I stutter. "I thought the greenhouse was…"

"The greenhouse is fine," she says sharply. Then she gets up and starts walking toward the back of the house. I'm supposed to follow, I guess, but suddenly I *really don't want to*. Suddenly I'm clenched with fear.

"It's right back here," she calls as her small figure fades into the darkness at the end of the hall.

I should leave. Right now. But I *can't*. It might save my life, but it wouldn't be *polite*. Which is crazy.

Gardens. Digging. *Bodies*, I find myself thinking.

The thing about my father in these situations is that he's *trained* to deal with them, plus he has the size and athleticism to handle himself. I don't.

As I'm frozen with indecision, I'm startled by a bright light coming from the end of the hallway. Mrs. McNamara calls, "Margo?"

And I can't help it; I walk down the hallway towards her. After all, she was my Sunday School teacher.

At the end of the hall, there's a right turn into a mudroom. I realize now that the light is coming from the open door to the green house. I take a deep breath and step into the light.

What immediately strikes me is the blaze of color; it's almost blinding. Orange and purple birds of paradise, a pink orchid, red peppers. And on the right, the rather tall, very healthy-looking pot plants.

In the middle of this rainbow brightness stands Mrs. McNamara, the sweet smile back.

"This is my crop," she says pleasantly. Proudly, I think.

I don't know what to say. Great-looking pot plants? I hesitate, but then she starts speaking again.

"Down in Lincoln, there's a wonderful hospice. People go there to die," she adds, in case I don't know what a hospice is.

"The staff there is fantastic, and includes my niece, Beth, of whom I'm very proud."

And now her eyes narrow, making this next a confrontation: "It's a great place, but nonetheless, every patient in there is *suffering*. They're nauseous, tired, and in pain. And there are properties in cannabidiol, which is—"

I interrupt her. "But you don't *sell* it to them, right?" I say, my own strength returning, now that I'm confident I won't be shot.

"Of course not!" responds Mrs. Mac, offended by the thought.

"Fine," I say. "Now *don't tell me anymore*. Because I was never here. Okay?"

It's something my dad might say. *Would* say, if he was in this situation.

A slight smile now from Mrs. Mac, followed by a nod.

I give her one last look, double-checking my instincts. Yes, this small, strong woman is not a killer. She's another tough Nebraska angel, doing what needs to be done. Just like June.

I apologize for taking up her time and go, leaving Mrs. McNamara in her Oz-like world of brilliant color.

Something lifts in me as I walk home. It feels good to take another suspect off the list. So freeing that, as I near home, I allow myself to open that compartment, the one that I sealed off after Boyd kissed me today.

When Dr. James hugged me earlier I felt like a kid again, free of everything. *Problem solved, now run along and play.*

But when Boyd kissed me I ricocheted right back to my present age, flailing, a riot of conflicting feelings. His kiss was…pretty convincing.

But I love Hank. So how can I?

These are my thoughts as I flop down on my bed, stare at the llama lamp.

When my mother died, there was so much confusion, so much commotion. So much *mothering* descended on me. My heart ached for her (and still does), but I was buoyed by a flood of cinnamon sweet rolls and hugs and tears and kindness. And by Hank. We were just friends then, just a nine- and ten-year-old, but something in his eyes said, "I'm here, I will catch you if you need me to." My friend, my soul twin, my future. And even though he's gone, I've somehow managed to keep him here, because I need him, so he's stayed. My Hank.

And that feels so much stronger than this whatever-it-is with Boyd.

I roll over and come face-to-face with Hank, lying on his side, head propped up on one arm.

I'm really glad to see him. Until he asks:

"So how was that kiss?"

FORTY-EIGHT

HANK

Margo's answer to my question was a jumble. She's conflicted and I *hate* that. Can't blame her, I guess, but it's still a *bitch* of a feeling. After an hour or so of hashing it out, I leave, looking for something to take my mind off the lead weight in my heart. I have to stay busy.

I've been meaning to check up on Sam Claypool, and when I do, I find him sitting in a patio chair staring at his pool. The pool's empty, a green pool cover stretched tight over it, a handful of autumn leaves dancing across the surface. Sam just stares, his face grim, intent.

I've come to spy on him because there's a chance that he'll be the next to go. His wife's odd choice of pet, her murmuring dark plans to her lover. Plus I have that feeling again—someone's going to die—and my money's on Sam.

I'm dying to read his mind, but that's not one of my new skills. There's something deep black in his stare, but it's not guilt, fear, or rage. Just extreme *focus*. He's trying to work something out.

After a few minutes, he gets up, heads into the house. I follow him.

Carolyn's not around, so I'm the only witness as Sam appears to ransack his own house. He goes through kitchen drawers, Carolyn's tote bag, a gym bag.

He finally ends up in the master bedroom going through Carolyn's closet, then her dresser. That's where he finds what he wants, in a lingerie drawer: a pack of cigarettes. He grips it, triumphant, clearly dying for a smoke, and is about to close the drawer when he stops cold. Stares. And then slowly, carefully, lifts a flat black square out of the drawer.

I know this object. It's June's diary.

Sam's puzzled, squinting at the book. But as soon as he opens it and reads a page, he knows. Drops the cigarettes, sits down hard on the bed.

Holy shitcakes, I think. It's *Carolyn*, not Sam.

As the realization sinks in that his wife is a murderer, Sam looks frightened, almost feminine. His hands flutter as he thumbs through the pages. He gently feels rough edges where a couple of pages have been torn out.

Finally the book falls to his lap and despair ripples across his face. He stands up awkwardly, his mind reeling, searching for his next move. Then almost falls over when the doorbell rings.

I pop outside to see who it is, and now it's my turn to freak: it's my mother. What the…?

Sam tries to compose himself, answers the door. When he sees who it is, he can barely mask his irritation. Mom, in her new odd uniform of shabby sweatpants and formal coat. Whatever she wants, this is *not* what he needs right now.

But the first words out of her mouth bring him right back into panic mode.

"Sam," she says, her voice surprisingly strong. "I've come to warn you about your wife."

Sam pulls her inside.

They don't even bother leaving the front hall, just face each other down right there. Sam opts to feign ignorance, which is a reach, considering the crazy in his eyes.

"What are you talking about?" he asks her.

"Your wife," she says again, as if she can't bear to utter the woman's name. "She's up to something. I don't know what it is, but I think you're in danger."

Sam almost faints with relief. *She doesn't know about the murder*, I can see him thinking.

"Emmie," he says, his strength returning. "I'm *fine*. You don't need to worry about me."

"Don't trust her, Sam," Mom insists, then repeats, "She's up to something."

Now a new look comes over Sam's face as he fixes my mom with a hard stare. "Where are you getting this?" he demands. "What do you know?"

Now Mom falters. She can't say she was hiding in his basement, spying. "I just know, okay? I'm telling you, she's *dangerous.*"

It's amazing how you can see the mental wheels spinning in someone's eyes, I think as I look at Sam. The calculation. Mindreading is unnecessary, I realize. I can see he's decided she's probably just a grieving crackpot, but he can't be too careful.

"Emmie," he says his voice equal parts reassurance and menace. "I appreciate your concern, but I'm *not* in danger. Look, I know how you feel about Carolyn, considering the history. But she's not dangerous. She's a good woman. A *school teacher.*"

Wow, I realize, he's gaslighting her. *Gaslight*—it's an old movie in which a treacherous man makes his suspicious wife thinks she's nuts. I'm almost proud when my mom sees through it.

"She is *not* a good woman, Sam," she almost spits. "I'm warning you."

The look in Sam's eyes now scares me: it's something like, *am I gonna have to take this crazy bitch out? Does she know too much?* I'm pretty sure that deep down he's just as cold-blooded as his wife.

The back door opens and shuts; both of them jump. Sam turns towards the sound and in an instant Mom's gone, out the door.

Thank God, I think.

Sam moves into the kitchen for a new showdown. He waits for his wife, diary in hand, as Carolyn comes up the back steps.

Here's what I notice: she sees him, sees the diary in his hands, and yet looks more confused than freaked. *Huh.*

"Hey…" she says warily.

"You goddamned bitch," he hisses in return. *Welcome home, honey.*

He lashes into her, his face reddening till he looks like a lobster in a pot.

"What did she have on you?" he growls. "Did she find out what you used to do? Who you used to be?"

Carolyn's eyelids blink helplessly as she tries to stutter a response. But Sam shuts her down.

"It's my fault, I guess. What did I think I was gonna do, rehabilitate you? The prettiest stripper at the skank club?"

Oh, I think. *This is news.*

"I gave you this house!" he thunders. "Put designer clothes on your ass! And *this* is what I get? You're not just a skank, you're a *murderer*?!"

"I don't know what you're talking about!" Carolyn shouts, and I believe her.

"Oh no?" Sam yells. "You *don't?* Then what was June Hudspeth's diary doing in your underwear drawer?"

Carolyn is completely panicked now, looking at the book Sam's brandishing. She does not recognize it—that's clear to me. But not to Sam.

Sam grabs her and pins her on the floor, hitting her with the diary.

"Do you know what you've done to me?" he bellows. "I had to cover up your disgusting past and now I have to hide your *murder*?!"

Bash—the book comes down hard across Carolyn's face. She's shivering, crying, trying to protect herself.

Get off her, I think. I don't like this woman, but for God's sake, don't batter her.

But Sam's relentless, his face pure fury.

"Well, I'm not covering for you anymore," he sneers. "You can go to jail for this, I don't care. You can go to hell!"

One last *bash* and he's off her, leaving her quivering on the kitchen floor.

But he *does* cover for her, or—more likely—for himself.

Because his next move is to take the diary outside and burn it in his firepit.

As I watch the book go up in flames, I think about popping over to Margo's, to tell her to somehow try and rescue it before it's gone. That's the clue bank right there, everything June was thinking about before her death.

But I don't. I don't want her anywhere near these people.

FORTY-NINE

MARGO

can't sleep. I don't know why I'm even trying. Something's bugging me. Why didn't Dr. James answer my question about Back-to-School Night? He *pivoted* like politicians do, sending the conversation in another direction. Was I really satisfied with his answer, or was I just desperate for things to go back to normal? For the chess pieces I've been toying with to go back to their proper places on the board?

I used to trust my gut, but now I'm not sure I do. I'm out of my depth, *plus* I'm still dating my dead boyfriend. Why should I trust me?

Hank pops into bed with me and I jump.

"Are you okay?" I ask immediately, still guilty about Boyd.

"No," he says. "But that's not important now. June's diary just showed up."

He tells me about the crazy scene over at the Claypools. About how Carolyn *looks* guilty, but maybe she's not.

I start to obsess about this new information and assume Hank is too. But when I look over, I see he's just staring at me.

"I need to know," he says again. "How did you feel when Boyd kissed you?"

I sigh. "Hank..."

"Look, he ambushed you, I know that. But you told him you couldn't be with him because I was still here. What if I wasn't?"

I look at him blankly, even though I know what he means. So he spells it out.

"If I wasn't here, would you hook up with Boyd?"

I don't answer immediately. I want to be sure.

"*No*," I finally say. And I mean it. "I really think this whole thing with Boyd is just about shared grief. *That's* the connection."

Hank's looking down now, trying to get something out.

"Because... what I really wanted to say is... *it's okay*. I'm *not* really here. Seeing you two together today... you're *alive*." Now he looks at me. "So it's okay, if it happens. You and Boyd."

I'm getting choked up, seeing how hard he's trying to do the right thing. But my resolve is firm.

"Hank," I tell him. "Boyd has always just been your little brother to me. That hasn't changed."

It's true. I can imagine lots of scenarios with Boyd, most of them involving heavy breathing. But I don't think we could ever have the profound connection I have with Hank. So it wouldn't be worth it.

Hank appears to accept this as the final word on the subject.

"You should try to get some sleep," he notes.

I nod and try to settle in. I'm certain I'll never sleep tonight, but I'm actually drifting off when I hear a sustained *PINGGGG!!!!* It's my laptop; a message—or several—has come in. I consider leaving it until morning, but I'm curious. I pad over to my desk and flip it on.

And there, lined up like soldiers, are about fifty messages from Cyber Salvage. Each with an attachment. I read the initial message aloud to Hank as he joins me at my desk. They've sent everything they recovered from June's computer.

But as I scroll through the attachments, I see that most of the files are corrupted. Lines and lines of computer gibberish interspersed with scraps of actual writing.

Police blotter notes like: *Found: a spare tire, located at 5th and Euclid. Appears to be off a pickup* and *tell Richard Minner he must obtain and post a building permit for his new deck!*

A note to remind Lance to *drive by Fletcher home at 31 N. Sycamore. Fletchers are away at daughter Jenny's wedding in Tulsa. Check on house.*

June, keeping everything in order, looking out for everyone in town. I keep scrolling; I feel like I'm digging for June herself amidst the cyber rubble. Hank and I find ourselves laughing and crying, reading June's little busybody notes aloud in her voice. I miss her, and I know Hank does too. I'm glad he's here.

It takes us hours to comb through the files; it's light out by the time we get to the last one.

And there, *finally*, is the name I've been looking for all night: *JoAnn.* Followed by more gibberish. I scan down quickly.

At the very end are two golden, completely legible lines: *After he drove her home, she never came back. Something must have happened. I'll ask him about it. I'll know by the look on his face.*

And that's the end of the last file. The last thing June ever typed on her computer, and—I believe—the reason she smeared blood on her monitor. The answer is somewhere in those four sentences.

"After he drove her home from what?" Hank asks me. I don't know. We're still puzzling over this when my alarm rings: time to get ready for school.

Hank pops out as I dress and head to school. I drift through my classes, there but not really.

So we've got a "he," which takes Emmie and Carolyn off the list. But then why was June's diary in Carolyn's drawer? Did Sam put it in there himself? I try to remember the specifics of Hank's Claypool story as I float into English class.

I see from the board that we're doing *Of Mice and Men* today. Good, I've already read that. I can zone out.

As Ted purrs on and on about George and Lennie, I fixate on the phrase *she never came back*. I should *know* this. *What did my mother never come back to?*

HANK

I go to the theater looking for answers. We're getting close. I can feel it. And the closer we get, the more danger Margo's in.

I need help. Some troubled spirit to drift down the stairs and unburden him or herself, clueing me in. Actually, I know *exactly* whose help I want.

"JoAnn Pierce!" I yell to the empty expanse. "I need your help! *Margo* needs you!"

Nothing. No sparkle at the top of the stairs, no fairy god-mother gliding down to help me.

I've gotten used to being powerless, but it was worth a try. For lack of a better idea, I start to poke around.

No one in the ladies' or men's rooms. I open the door to the theater: nothing but the low-lit sconce lights along the walls.

I momentarily wonder if I could sit down and *will* an image to come up on the screen. Watch Margo at school, maybe. But since I have the option to actually pop into school, that doesn't seem very productive. I close the door.

What else? I peek into the ticket booth. There's a stool, an old green ticket roll, an empty cash box. Nothing of interest.

I'm about to give up and start playing some blues guitar when I spot one door I've never tried. It's in a little hallway that crosses behind the theater. I walk over and gently turn the knob. It opens.

Inside, there's a short flight of stairs up to darkness. I stand there for a moment, suddenly anxious. I don't want to go up there, and I'm not sure why.

But I'm not accomplishing anything in the lobby, so I find the light switch and flip it on. A faint blue glow appears at the top of the stairs.

I don't like this. This is creepy. But I go up the stairs, and find myself in the theater's projection booth. *Of course!* Makes sense. Nothing to be anxious about.

There's a great old-time movie projector on a stand. I know this machine; we had one like this at a rickety old camp where I used to work. I was in charge of movie night, and I'd make the kids watch classics like *High Noon* and *Shane*. They'd grumble at first—they wanted *Despicable Me* or whatever—but then they'd get sucked in.

I give the take-up reel a spin. This is *cool*.

The back wall is lined with shelves of movie reel cases. I move closer to see what movies they have. This could be amazing.

But when I read the labels, there are no movie titles, just names: *Burt Jacobson, Lorelei Adams, Marie Randolph.*

Huh. I keep reading. *Karen Malesky, Mary Minner*—wait, I know that name. She was the church organist who died a few years ago. As I read more, I realize I know several of these names. All local, all deceased. I check one of the cases: yes, there's a film reel in there. *These are movies of people's lives*, I conjecture. And immediately, I want to find mine. I lean in, searching: *Thomas Kelly, Jerry Krupnick...* I'm skimming now, looking for *James*.

I don't find it, but I find another name that roots me to the spot.

JoAnn Pierce.

FIFTY-ONE

MARGO

Ted's droning on about Curley and his wife. I forget who these characters are in the book; I'd better check in. As he continues, I start to remember: It's set on a California ranch during the Great Depression. The main characters are migrant farm workers. George and Lennie are friends; George is small but smart, Lennie is feeble-minded but massive and strong. Curley's the mean boss, and his pretty wife flirts with all the guys.

"What do you think Curley and his wife represent in the story?" Ted asks us.

Don't look at me.

Jenn Duffy's got her hand up, God bless her. Ted calls on her.

"Oppression of the worker," says Jenn. "Curley uses his superior position to oppress the men, his wife uses her sexual power."

Someone's been reading SparkNotes. Ted beams: "*Great*, Jenn! Oppression bordering on *evil*, right? Have you ever known someone like that, who uses their position to intimidate a community?"

Oh *yes, yes*, everyone's known someone like that. The class discussion takes off, the teacher's happy. Good, I can get back to *my* work.

I try to think what group or committee my mom abandoned. Not the town council; she went to a meeting there the night she died. Not Garden Club, she loved that. Something at church? She and June went to the same church.

As I ponder, my gaze lands on Ty Cloninger's copy of *Of Mice and Men*. The jacket cover is a picture of George and Lennie from behind, sitting together under a tree by a river. We have the same copy at home, my mom...

I lean back. *That's it. My mom quit her book club.* I remember now. When I was eight-ish, she stopped going. I asked her about it; she brushed it off. Said she was too busy.

Book club met at a different house every other month, so someone could easily have driven her home. But a man? There were no men in book club. Someone's husband, maybe?

"Why is Lennie attracted to Curley's wife?" Ted is asking. "Was it her kindness? Was she a kindred spirit? Or was it just straight-up sexual attraction?"

Ted loves to talk about sex in books. Easy way to keep teenagers' attention.

"He just likes soft things," says Jenn Duffy.

FIFTY-TWO

HANK

I have to watch this movie. If it's about JoAnn's life, maybe it'll also show her death.

My hands are shaking, but I manage to set up the reel. *Loop the film through till it catches, turn the light on.* The machine starts to whir. Through the little viewing window, I can see white on the screen, then numbers.

I head down the stairs and go into the theater. The house lights are dimming as I take my seat. When the image appears, it's hard to make out at first. It's dark and it's snowing.

But as my eyes adjust, I realize I'm looking at the town hall parking lot. Two figures emerge from the old red brick building; two women in parkas. I recognize one of them: it's JoAnn, in blue. The infamous blue parka she died in.

As she says goodbye to the other woman and starts to walk in the snow, it dawns on me: *She's leaving the town council on the night she died.*

I lean back, my mind a whirl. *These aren't movies of people's lives; these are death reels.*

I grip my armrests. Suddenly I feel like a kid at a movie that's too scary for me. I want my dad here with me. But I keep watching.

JoAnn trudges up the road towards home. The snow is getting heavier now, and she's leaning into the wind. There's no audio, but I can almost hear the gusts blowing by her. She slips and has to steady herself. Then suddenly, she's illuminated by headlights.

She looks up; the blue of her parka is electric in the bright light. A car pulls up next to her. The passenger window rolls down; JoAnn leans forward.

I can't make out the car and find myself straining to see better.

JoAnn seems to be kindly declining the offer of a ride while wind whips the fur of her hood. I feel like I want to warn her not to get in, but the weather is *insanely* bad. Finally, she gives in and gets into the car.

As the car drives away from the camera, I actually stand up, trying to see the make of the car, the license plate, anything. But the car disappears into the snow.

"Who is that?" I yell to no one.

FIFTY-THREE

MARGO

'm eight years old. I'm in our kitchen wearing my snowflake pajamas. I'm excited; Mom has let me stay up to pass the snacks at her book club. I've helped her to arrange cheese, crackers, and grapes on a tray.

I follow her into the living room; she swishes ahead of me in a maroon velvet skirt. There's a fire in the fireplace. The club members are there, talking and laughing.

I take my tray over to the couch first, to Emmie James and Sue Cloninger. They smile, thank me, fuss over my cute pj's. Then over to June, in the chair by the fire. She winks at me, helps herself to cheese and crackers. Then Zhen Chang, on the other side of the fireplace. She's polite, a bit more subdued than the others. I remember Mom saying she came to book club to work on her English. Then...who? A couple of church ladies maybe? Vivi Byard and Liz Fletcher? I think so.

Then Beth Earley, club president, half-glasses on, going over her notes for the meeting.

Something is bothering me; I suddenly feel self-conscious. I stiffen as I take the tray to the chair by the window. Who is it? I hold out the tray; a hand reaches out. I make eye contact with a handsome young man. He smiles at me—a dazzling, disarming smile. Ted Hawkins.

I jolt upright in my chair. My mind careens from Memory Ted to Present Day Ted across the classroom. He sees the look on my face; there's a long, silent corridor of connection between us.

He breaks it, asking me: "What do *you* think, Margo? Did Lennie mean to kill Curley's wife?"

Just my heartbeat now, banging like a bass drum.

"*No*," I answer hoarsely. "He didn't know his own strength."

After a moment, betraying nothing, Ted blinks.

The buzzer rings; class is over. I try to get to the door but it's lunchtime, there's a bottleneck to get out.

Ted stops me, asks me to stay. *My mother's killer wants to get me alone.* I stay, but remain where I'm standing, a few feet from the door. Ted settles himself on the edge of his desk. Says I seem distracted, asks me how I'm doing. I haven't come to the school paper meetings. He's *kind*, and suddenly doubt creeps back in. Was he really in book club or did I imagine that? I've been up all night, after all.

I mumble barely passable answers to his questions. Finally he lets me go, after resting a reassuring hand on my shoulder. A Soul Brother touch.

At lunch, Delia has no idea if Ted was in book club, but she's intrigued by the theory.

"It *works*," she says. "Your mom quit the club, maybe after he drove her home one night. He probably made a pass at her; the guy's a walking hormone."

I'm starting to melt into my mac and cheese. Sleep deprivation, plus shock, plus confusion. But Delia has my back; she steers me to my next class, says she'll meet me after school.

Walking me home, Delia insists we tell my dad. Have him get the Omaha Major Crimes unit on this.

We go up to his bedroom, now a sick room, and try to rouse him. But he's deeply lethargic, his brain a snarl of statins and barbiturates. He doesn't even recognize the name Ted Hawkins; he thinks we're talking about a basketball player.

Delia assesses the situation, and I'm so grateful for her presence of mind, I want to cry. I sit and hold Dad's hand while she goes downstairs to get the phone. She's going to call Omaha PD herself.

Dad's out of it, but he can see I'm upset. He gives my hand a faint squeeze.

"It'll be okay, baby," he mumbles. "I'll take care of it."

Now I do cry. *It'll be okay.* I *so* want to believe him.

I hear Delia talking, then a loud *thump*. Then nothing. *Weird.*

"Delia?" I call. No answer. I head downstairs.

I round the curve of the landing and can see through the front hall arch into the living room. And what I see is Delia's legs, flat on the floor. Not moving.

FIFTY-FOUR

HANK

feel sick as I continue to watch the movie. The car is pulled over now and the driver is assaulting JoAnn. There's too much winter outerwear to tell who he is, and no audio. I think about going up to the booth to try to get the audio on, but I can't move.

JoAnn is trying to fend off her attacker, but he's holding her wrists. She seems more angry than scared, yelling at him.

She *knows* him, I realize. This is no drifter.

She manages to get one arm free, opens the door and tumbles out into the snow. The driver lunges after her. The image cuts to outside: two figures battling in a blizzard.

JoAnn heaves upwards and lurches away from the car. Behind her, I recognize the linden tree on Route 57. The shrine site. It won't be long now.

The driver grabs for JoAnn, catches her hood. She twists around and falls backward, going down hard.

The driver clambers on top of her but doesn't try to undress or further assault her. Instead he clasps her hands; he appears to be pleading with her.

Now a close-up of JoAnn staring upwards, a startled expression on her face. She looks so much like Margo, I catch my breath. But something's off, her expression is fixed in place, her eyes don't move.

Now I see the large rock her head is resting on, the blood pooling under her hair.

She's not just startled; she's *gone*.

Now the shot finally reverses to the attacker, revealing what I think I've known for the last few minutes. It's Ted, his eyes wild, half-blinded by snow. But realizing, realizing.

His jaw falls open and I see the *realest* expression I've ever seen on this guy's face: *utter agony*. He sits back on his heels and screams silently up at the relentless sky. Holds her hands one last time, kisses them. Then stands up, makes his way around to the driver's door. Gets in and drives off.

No light now, just a dark splotch in the snow by the side of a road.

The screen fades to back. The movie's over.

As the house lights come up to a soft glow, I sit and collect myself.

It was Ted all along. Accidentally killing a woman he clearly loved. Then June, when she found out. Then trying to frame Carolyn with the diary; easy, he certainly knew his way around the Claypool house. Ted Hawkins, who was in the car when his girlfriend plowed into me. The guy's got some serious blood on his hands.

I'm gripped with an instinct to tail him, to *see* him, now that I know. I pop to his house, into his room. He's not there.

I'm about to pop out when something catches my eye. A trick of the late afternoon light, a golden twinkle on Ted's dresser. I move closer: it's a bottle of men's cologne with a wooden stopper. *Chesapeake*.

As I stare at it, panic clenches my chest. Because suddenly I know where Ted is. I can *feel* it. He's with Margo.

FIFTY-FIVE

MARGO

I run to Delia. I assume she must have fainted, probably because I feel like fainting myself. I don't see him until I reach her. Ted, sitting on our ottoman, holding a long screwdriver. He looks at me as I enter.

"She wasn't supposed to be here," he says. "It's *you* I want to talk to."

I look at him, then at Delia, then at the screwdriver. I've stepped into surreal world and have absolutely *no* idea what to do.

"Is she okay?" I ask nonsensically, as if Ted's on my side.

"You look so much like your mother," he says. "It's uncanny."

Now I feel the danger. Now the cop blood starts to pulse through my veins.

"I need to see if she's breathing," I tell Ted, though I'm really asking for his permission.

He waves me away with the screwdriver. "She'll be fine," he insists.

That's how he got in, I realize. I always lock the doors now. *He jimmied the lock with the screwdriver.*

"I need you to *understand*," Ted continues. "We're so much alike. I lost my mother too. And we *both* lost yours."

I'm stiffening now; I can't stand hearing him talk about my mother.

"I know how much she meant to you," he says, "because she meant that much to me. Do you understand that?"

I wish I had a gun. I want to *nuke* this guy.

"My dad's upstairs," I tell him.

"Margo," he says. "Your dad's not well enough to go to work. So that's not much of a threat, is it?" He sounds like a teacher urging logic, which infuriates me.

"Why are you here?" I ask him.

He weighs this, then softly replies, "To make you *understand*."

"Okay," I respond. "Make me understand."

"Your mom gave me *books*," he says. "When my mom was sick. The other women brought food; your mom brought Conrad, Kipling. She *talked* to me. She gave me what I *needed*. We understood each other. *That's* why I came back after college. When you have someone like that, a *soulmate*, you don't give up."

I feel the vitriol spewing up inside me. So many things I want to yell at him, *"What the hell do you know about soulmates?!"* being the first. But I'm too angry to speak. I try to keep my voice steady.

"Ted," I say. "I need to call an ambulance, get Delia checked out. You can leave if you want to; I'll just say she tripped. I know you didn't mean to hurt her."

Ted looks confused now, worlds away, like he doesn't know who I'm talking about.

"Of course I didn't mean to hurt her. I *loved* your mother," he says. "I was just trying to explain myself to her that night, tell her how I *felt*. When I saw her walking, I thought: *This is it. This was meant to happen.* But she wouldn't listen. She tried to get away and she hit her head. Is that my fault?!"

So that's what happened. I can't be any kind of cop now. I need to sit down. I plop into the chair by the fireplace. The anger balloon has popped and all I feel is a terrible sadness.

Ted crosses over and kneels in front of me.

"You believe me, don't you?" he pleads. "I would *never* have hurt her."

He takes my hand and I can't even pull it away. I'm so tired suddenly. Completely powerless.

I hear a voice behind me. "Margo," Hank says. "Run out the front door. Go get help."

I don't look at him. Instead, I look at Ted.

"And June?" I say. "Was that an accident too?"

"She caught me off guard," he mutters.

"So you shot her. Bit of an impulse control problem, I'd say."

I've gone too far; Ted's expression devolves into a stark glare. He pulls an arm back and slaps me across the face, hard. He's here, the man who's capable of murder. He's knocked my head backwards; I look up and see Hank.

"*Go,*" he says.

Ted and the front door are to my right. I bolt left, rocketing toward the back door. I burst outside, gulp the cool air. Then I'm running, across the backyard and into the fields beyond. I know I'm going the wrong way; there's nothing but farmland in front of me. But the adrenaline is pumping, telling me to *just run.*

I dare a look behind me and my heart sinks. There he is, his white shirt billowing lavender in the dusky light as he runs after me. His loping stride twice as long as mine. *Maybe I can make it to the Andersons' farmhouse,* I think, and turn on the speed.

And that's what does me in. I'm moving so fast, I don't account for a deep tractor rut in my path. And then I'm down, my ankle twisted, heaving as I flail in the ditch.

When he reaches me he kneels on my legs, holds me down with a hand to the shoulder.

"I didn't mean to kill her," he says breathlessly. "Don't you *get* that?"

He's got me pinned but there's one thing I can do. I throw back my head and scream.

But Ted Hawkins really does have an impulse control problem, and before I know it, he's stabbed the screwdriver deep into my chest.

FIFTY-SIX

HANK

've had dreams like this, where I can't get to Margo in time to save her, and now it's happening. I couldn't stop Ted from catching her, couldn't stop him from pinning her down, couldn't stop him from stabbing her.

And now she's lying there bleeding, a look of shock on her face, while Ted cleans off his screwdriver. Tucks in his shirt. Then starts to walk calmly back towards the street.

It's still light but a bright moon has come out as Ted leaves Margo to die.

I'll see her soon, I think sadly, *at the theater.* I crouch beside her, wishing I could at least hold her hand as she passes. Make it easier for her somehow.

I see a pair of eyes in the distance. Down low, coming towards us. Not human—it's a coyote. It can smell something dying.

I jump to my feet, wave my arms, scream at it to get the hell away. And here's the thing: *it does*. It stops, turns tail, and slinks off down another tractor rut. It *sensed* me.

And then I realize: I'm *not* helpless. Margo is halfway to the netherworld, and this is where I can actually be of some use. I've done it before.

I climb on top of her, yell her name. Her spirit eyes pop open: wild, confused, just like her dad's.

But it's *not* just like her dad because suddenly we're touching and it's like an electric switch has been thrown. I can hold her again, *finally*, my Margo. My *girl*. I can *have her back*.

It feels *so good*, her spirit self clutching me. But her eyes are darting around, panicked.

Which makes me realize that I can't do it. I'm not here to escort her to the afterlife. I have to help her to *live*.

"Margo," I say, pushing her down. "You have to get back into your body. It's not time for you to go yet."

She clutches me harder and I remember how strong she is. It's agonizing because I want this too. I want us to be together.

But I love her, and there's only one thing to do: I peel her hands away and push her into her body, gently but firmly.

And here's where I really almost crack, because she's in pain now, her body spasming from the loss of blood. She reaches one arm up towards me, desperate for rescue.

I'm just about to give in when I hear a shout behind me: "*Margo!*" It's Roy, stumbling out the back door. He sees her, he heard her scream, *he's coming to save her*. I fall to my knees; I always knew he was Superman! But he's ambling slowly, still dazed by meds, less like Superman than a bear just out of hibernation. I look at Margo and will him to move faster. He's halfway to us when Ted reappears. There's a shovel leaning against a garden fence; he grabs it.

I yell a warning to Roy, and I could swear he hears me, because at the last minute he dodges; the shovel misses his head and catches him in the back. Probably just ingrained cop reflexes. Either way, he goes down like an oak tree. And then Ted's on top of him, pummeling him. As I watch, I see the hatred in Ted's fists, the fury of a man who lost someone he thought was his soulmate to another guy.

But luckily there's a stronger power at work here, the power of a man's love for his daughter. Because suddenly, like a man restraining a hyper kid, Roy grips Ted's arms and holds them in place. Then flips Ted on to his back and uses his bulk to dominate him.

I feel a brief victory surge, but when I look back at Margo, I realize it might be too late. She's not moving anymore and her sweater is saturated with blood.

I look back at Roy, who has managed to retrieve a cell phone from his pocket. But here's where his weakness and torpor undo him: he drops it. Then reaches for it, which gives Ted a chance to grab the shovel and *smash* him on the side of the head. Roy falls to the ground.

As Ted gets up, the last man standing as night encroaches, I think of a class he taught last year on the novel *No Country for Old Men.* The conclusion of his lecture: "Sometimes evil triumphs over good."

And here, as a late September chill purples the sky, that's how it feels. Margo, Roy, Delia, all good, all down. And Ted, picking up the shovel. He holds it up high over Roy, ready to dispatch his rival.

And then, mercifully, justice pierces the twilight with a single gunshot. Ted drops the shovel and collapses.

It's hard to see all the way to the street, but I can tell from his stature that the last man standing is now Deputy Lance Ritter.

There are four ambulances to choose from, but I ride in Margo's. Talking to her all the way as the medics work on her. Re-telling random old Hank/Margo stories: "Remember how we watched that show on the Dark Ages, then wanted to start a metal band called the Visigoths? But none of us could play anything?" and "Remember when we rode the Fireball at the state fair and threw up our fried Snickers bars?"

The crazier the better, I think. Anything to keep her conscious. I can't tell whether she can hear or see me, but at one point she murmurs something.

I lean in: "What's that, honey?" I urge her. I can barely hear her whisper: "June loved birds."

She's staring at something in the distance. I follow her gaze and see—through the ambulance's back window—a flock of snow geese flying away.

There is nothing good about this night. And yet, at the hospital, it calms me to see my father in field general mode. All except Delia are in critical care, tended by ER docs, but they're all Dad's patients so he consults on each case. Even Ted.

Delia, just concussed, is the first to recover, and so the first to tell what she knows to Norfolk police (and Lance, who apparently doesn't know anything, except that Ted was about to kill his hero). I'm at her side, cheering her on as she centers the crosshairs on Ted.

Ted, I don't give a crap about. I hope he dies. Then I can school *him* a little, when he arrives at the theater.

Roy's in bad shape, but the doctors seem confident in his recovery.

This is not the case in Margo's suite, where faces are solemn and words are few. When a doctor has to dismiss a nurse for crying onto the operating table, I know things are bad.

I leave the room and suddenly find myself in an unlikely Hank spot: the hospital chapel. On my knees, head bowed. A ghost praying for the living.

FIFTY-SEVEN

MARGO

drift in and out of sleep. The walls in this place are golden, sparkly. Is this the hospital or Heaven?

I turn to the person next to me and see big brown eyes, a reassuring smile. It's my mother.

I guess I'm in Heaven after all.

I reach out for her, hug her, crying. "*Mom*," I sob. "Am I dead?"

"No," she says kindly. "You're still alive."

I hold myself away so I can look at her. "But then... why are you here?" I ask her.

"You needed me," she says simply.

I hug her again, tears flowing. There's so much I want to tell her. Ask her.

"Mom," I say. "Ted Hawkins tried to kill me. Like he killed you."

"I know," she says sadly. Then adds firmly: "But *you lived*."

"*Yeah*," I say back and we both smile. Her eyes lock into mine; I feel her warmth envelop me. Wherever I am, it sure feels like Heaven.

"Oh God, Mom, I miss you *so much*," I tell her.

She reaches out, smooths my hair. "I'm always with you," she says.

We're both crying now, but it's okay. We're *together*.

"Margo," she says. "There's something I have to tell you. Something hard."

No. I don't want anything hard. I just want this moment to last forever.

"You need to let Hank go," she says. "It's time."

And as she says it I remember: *That's what she told me in the shoe store dream.*

Now the pain in my heart is back, the heavenly sparkle is gone.

"I *can't*," I tell her, crying again.

"Yes you can, honey," she says, then leans in and kisses me on the forehead. "I love you," she says, and I know she's leaving.

Now the pain consumes me.

"*No!!*" I scream, reaching out for her. She's gone, but I hear another voice saying my name. My eyes focus: a nurse in pink scrubs with warm brown eyes sits next to me.

"Try to get some sleep, honey," she says.

I'm in the hospital. My mom's gone, but I'm alive.

FIFTY-EIGHT

HANK

eacher arrested in old/new murders... English teacher killed mother, chief's wife and sec'y... Hinterlands Homicide.

These are some of the crawls that accompany the coverage of the murders on TV news. I've been watching it with my family. It's funny how even when something is happening in your hometown, everyone goes home to watch it on TV.

The mood in the James household is clearly one of relief. It's borderline *festive*: Dad has made nachos for everyone to eat in front of the TV. Ghost Mom is gone; she seems energized by this news binge, analyzing the facts like her old self. And Boyd is actually *speaking*, tossing in comments like "I always knew there was something off about him," which may or may not be true. But it doesn't matter; they're a family again.

There's a new lightness between my parents; it's clear a burden has been lifted. I'm not coming back, nor are June or Jo-Ann, but at least the puzzle is *solved*. I actually wonder if they may have suspected each other, which can't be good for a marriage. I know my dad must have suspected my mom at least a *little*. That has to be why he replaced the distinctive Russian ammo in their little pistol with the Walmart ammo—to cover for her, just in case she was the shooter. Which is a pretty intense kind of love; being willing to cover for your grief-crazy wife. Not like Dad but also *so* like him: doing what he thought needed to be done to protect his family. A man who's seen a lot of death and knows it doesn't reverse itself, determined to protect the living.

As for the Russian ammo... I'm willing to let it float downstream, like Dad did. My guess, and final word on the subject: he bought it because it was on sale.

Anyway, all seems well with the Jameses, which is f-ing *awesome*.

In Lazarus as a whole though, I can finally grasp the meaning of the phrase "media circus." It really is like the circus is in town: brightly colored journalists scampering from coffee shop to high school to hospital, their TV vans creating Lazarus's first-ever traffic jams.

Delia's a celebrity, which is a coup for her parents' restaurant; she grants interviews over steamed dumplings and pork fried rice.

Carolyn is a media favorite—not because anyone knows about the affair, but because she's both Ted's colleague and a camera-ready babe. Her new TV star status is compounded by the fact that her husband has bought her a new Porsche; a mea culpa for beating the crap out of her, I suppose.

And something really festive, something that actually made me laugh out loud, was a recent visit to the Nordgrens. I don't like loose ends, and neither does Margo. I wanted to find out where their new car/sapphire money came from. It took close inspection of the house but I finally found it, in a little frame on what must be Linda's bedside table. A Nebraska Lottery scratch-off worth $50,000.

Of course! My faith in my judgement of character is restored. Midwesterners of Scandinavian descent *would not* flaunt, or even tell anyone about, a sudden influx of cash. It would be *unseemly*, plus someone might ask for a handout. Al Nordgren is firmly back where he belongs: poker-faced behind the cash register at Marcy's.

There's so much going on, and I'm frankly a little pissed that I'm not alive to cover all this myself. I could have been the youngest-ever Pulitzer Prize winner, ironically using the journalistic tools I learned from the murderer himself. Oh well. That's actually pretty far down on my list of Life Regrets.

Which brings me to Margo. She's still in the hospital, but pretty well patched up now. I spent several long nights lying beside her, quieting her nightmares as she processed what happened with Ted. We're actually closer than we've ever been after this latest ordeal. Lying eye to eye, talking it out a little at a time as her punctured lung heals.

She wants so badly to be back in action; I think she wants to be the detective, prosecutor, and jailer in this case. I tell her she needs to focus on healing, which just aggravates her. I feel for her, which is why I'm doing the footwork for her, more or less.

Today I'm down the hall in Ted's room as the Omaha Major Crimes unit interrogates him. I'm inclined to hate these guys. Where were they when a teenager was trying to solve this case on her own? But now that all of western media has descended on Lazarus, here they are, all jacketed up and ready to grill.

"If it was an accident, why didn't you tell anyone?" asks the lead guy.

Ted—awkwardly angled in his torso bandages and handcuffs—looks pained when he talks about JoAnn.

I marvel at the plasticity of his face. Now, and when he was able to shoot June, then drive to Back-to-School Night and charm the moms. He acts the sorrowful spurned lover now, gripped with remorse at his actions.

When Omaha asks him why he killed June, he repeats, "She caught me off guard," as if it was a reasonable response. Apparently the question of why he was packing is beside the point. This is Nebraska, after all. But the important thing is *he said it*. He murdered June and they know he tried to kill Margo, so off to Leavenworth he goes.

As he details June's request to see him, his rage at her accusation and his satisfaction at pulling the trigger—"She deserved it," he snarls—I revise my assessment: he's a psychopath, but not a crafty one. His obvious pride in avenging his mother and destroying his father—all being videotaped—won't save him any time in Leavenworth.

After an hour or so, the cops are satisfied with what they have. They whisper a mini-conference. I eavesdrop and am pleased to hear that the lead guy wants to honor a formality: they will bring Roy in in his wheelchair to make the formal arrest. And Margo too, at Roy's request. Roy knows who solved the case.

Everything seems so wrapped up that I'm completely caught off guard by what happens next.

FIFTY-NINE

MARGO

'm alive again. I can't remember everything, but I feel like I've traveled between life and death many times in the past few days. Did I want to cross over permanently and join Hank and Mom? Maybe I did. But here I am in my hospital bed, bandaged and sore, monitors purring. My sweet nurse, Lola, fusses over me.

I don't think I'm ready to feel everything yet; I'm in some form of shock, I guess. Plus I've been busy; the visitors just keep coming.

Emmie James came by with these incredible apple walnut muffins she makes; I've always loved them. From the minute she sat down, I knew she was *back*: the direct gaze, the hearty laugh, the kind intelligence. We talked about what Hank would have thought of all this, which required some bluffing on my part; I *know* what he thinks. Just seeing the life in her eyes made me want to leave this bed, but I'm not allowed yet.

Dr. James checks in almost every day. The first time he stopped in, he had an embarrassed look on his face, like something was bothering him. When he finally let loose, he started with "I never answered your question." It took us a minute to get to what question he was referring to, the one about why he wasn't at Back-to-School Night. His belated answer came out in the form of a burdened confession:

"I'm a *doctor*, a witness to life and death. I understand the unfairness of nature, of events, and—usually—I accept them. But back in September, just two months after..." He didn't have to tell me what happened in July. His expression turned wretched, his lips taut. "I *could not bring myself to be in the same room with that woman*, not unless I really had to. So I stayed home."

I know who he's referring to and can hear his guilt about not being able to remain an objective man of science, under *all* circumstances. Which is impossible. I go in for a hug but he stops me. "Your stitches." He smiles, glad to have that confession out, I think.

Lance came by, which was intense. We've never really had a relationship, but now he's saved my life—and Dad's—which is a new kind of connection.

I started to apologize to him for blurting out the truth about his birth, but he waved me silent. He had a lot to say; it was like he was stepping into a confession booth.

"I've always been a coward," he started, and I caught my breath. His whole life story came out: how hard his adoptive father was on him. Thought he was inept, called him a wimp. They had a big blowout the day Lance's parents died in the plane crash.

Lance's father had wanted him to learn to fly, but Lance was scared. He refused to go up with them that day, and then was devastated when the plane crashed. Thought it was somehow his fault for being a coward.

That's why he joined the police force: to overcome his fears and be a hero. He found new family in June and my parents, and was devastated at losing first Mom, then June. But when he learned that June was his real mother, how devoted she was to him, he found his strength. He worked the case, cruised every neighborhood in town, learned to shoot, *really* shoot, at something besides video game zombies. That's how he was able to save me and finally be a hero.

I can never repay him, but I do have one thing to offer: Hank's message from Lance's adoptive mother. I told Lance the lie I had concocted: that I went to a psychic when I was trying to solve the murder. That's how the message came through. He was so moved he grabbed my hand and just held it; we sat that way for a long time in my hospital room.

Delia's been here every day. Today she came by with Boyd, which was an interesting turn of events. A bit awkward at first, but by the end we were roaring with laughter. Delia got in bed with me and started doing the last scene from *The Wizard of Oz*—"and you were there, and you and you..." in the voice of our overly-aggressive gym teacher, who tends to shout everything. She really let it rip, and by the time she got to "There's no place like home!" my chest wound hurt from laughing.

We became kids again, and it was like this strange romantic episode between me and Boyd never happened. Just the kids we used to be, goofing around in a grown-up place.

My most regular companion has been my fellow sickie, Dad. He's out of bed already, and his meds have been sorted out, which is good news and bad news. Good because he seems more like his old self, and bad because he feels this monumental guilt for leaving me to solve the crime on my own.

I've told him he has to stop apologizing. He's always had my back; now I had a chance to have his. But he's still troubled by it, and I'm still reeling from everything that's happened. I also think we're both at the beginning of a new stage of mourning, now that Mom's killer's been discovered, but I'm not ready to go there yet. So we've been playing a lot of gin rummy and, of course, Five Letter Word.

In fact, that's what we're doing when the OMC guy comes to take us to Ted's room. They're offering Dad the courtesy of making the official arrest. I see Dad's chin go up, shifting into professional mode, though he's not allowed to get out of his wheelchair.

As they wheel us down the hall, I'm seized with dread at facing the monster behind the door. Dad wants me there; I think he feels like he doesn't really deserve credit for this arrest himself.

When we're actually in the room with Ted, I just want to go back to my bed, let the pros handle this. But here I am and there he is, my former English teacher, shackled and bandaged. Taking everything in, trying to calculate if there's any way he can still charm his way out of this.

Dad is stoically doing his job, and the two OMC guys in the room are just standing there like sentries. But the vibe is tense; I can feel that these two adversaries—Ted and Dad—want to *spring* at each other again and fight to the death.

So it's a total shock when the real craziness comes from outside, literally bursting through the door. Gib Hawkins, bloodshot, rumpled, but tough as leather, with a shotgun aimed at his son.

The OMC guys and Lance immediately spring into action, aiming their weapons at Gib. I look to Dad for authority and quickly realize: *He doesn't care.* It takes a lot for Dad not to put the rule of law first. But if Ted Hawkins gets mowed down by his own father? *Great.* Less paperwork.

I'm surprised when I hear my own voice, directed at Gib: "You don't want to do this."

It sounds ridiculous even as I say it. Clearly he *does* want to do this.

"He's your *son*," I add, not wanting to see more blood.

"I have no son," spits Gib.

And just like that, I have the answer: "Yes you do," I tell him. "*Lance* is your son. Yours and June's."

Stunned, Gib lowers his rifle. Which allows the cops to restrain him. Gib doesn't seem to notice; he's just looking at Lance, amazed.

I realize Dad's looking at me and remember I haven't told him.

It seems like a lie is necessary, so I offer one: "I found the birth certificate in her house."

I'll deal with this later—a minor lie to bolster a major truth.

As the cops try to sort out what to do with Gib, I catch Ted's eye. The facade is gone and he's scrambling again. He thought he could eviscerate his father by killing June, but he never thought he'd be *replaced.* He'll be locked up, and Gib will have a new son.

As I lock eyes with him, I almost smile. *You took my mother, my boyfriend, and my friend, but you didn't win after all, did you, Ted?*

SIXTY

HANK

'm watching something beautiful. The sun is up, ash gray has morphed into a peachy pink, and Margo has slept through the night. No nightmares, no anxious muttering, just sound, heavy sleep. Just like I promised her.

She's home now, back in her room with the vintage fashion posters and concert stub collage, where she belongs. Still bandaged, still stiff, but getting stronger every day.

The *Omaha World Herald* and even the *Chicago Tribune* have sent reporters to interview the girl who solved her mother's murder. Margo was a pro, giving them the plucky schoolgirl they wanted for their stories, but making sure her dad got credit too. And she actually has fans now: people have come from as far as Tucson to meet her. Roy finally had to turn them away.

But that was all mid-week; it's Saturday now and Margo's resting. And as nice as it is to lie here and watch her sleep the sleep of the angels, something inside me is uneasy.

Because deep down, I know that by helping Margo solve the case, I've made myself superfluous. We can both move on now, but I'm not ready.

Looking around her room at all the Hank/Margo memorabilia, I'm getting choked up with nostalgia. The picture from our camping trip, where our only matches got wet and we had to pretend it was fun telling ghost stories by flashlight in the cold tent. The stuffed koala bear she won for herself at the state fair that we pretended *I* won for her. The 8 x 10 black-and-white picture she took of me during her photography phase, where I look cooler than I ever have in real life.

Something about that flat gray image reminds me of my current existence: here, but not in the flesh.

The sunrise on this calmer, happier Lazarus makes me yearn so much I could throw up. I want to *stay*. I want it all back.

I'm getting so worked up that when I first hear the bell ring, I think it's just part of my emotional overload. But as it continues—*ding... ding... ding...*—I realize it's not coming from me. It's *calling* me, and I know where. I pop over to the theater.

The bar is back, and the bartender. He's waiting for me, ringing a bell. When he sees me, he puts it down.

"Last call, Hank," he says.

I know what he means, but I resist. I don't cross over to him. I just stand there.

"*No*," I say.

He sighs, unsurprised. "There's nothing more for you to do. It's time to go."

"But she still needs me," I lie. And then, more truthfully: "And I need *her*."

"You've already had more time to say goodbye than most people get," he counters.

I've always been a diplomat, and now I negotiate with all I've got. "I know it's time to go," I say. "I get it. But just give me a day to wrap things up. Just *one day*. To say a final goodbye."

The bartender gives me a hard look. "You've got one hour," he says.

I can tell there's no wiggle room here, so I thank him and immediately pop back to Margo. I gently wake her up and tell her to drive over to the river. She knows where. She sees the urgency in my eyes and gets right up.

Now I pop over to the James house and see a sight that softens some of the heartbreak: Mom and Boyd having breakfast together. Talking, *connecting* with a new closeness. A mother and son, not a mother and her *other* son. *They'll be all right*, I realize.

I've got tears in my eyes as I pop out and see my dad doing yardwork. As I watch him work, his lined face focused, I understand: *This guy has survived a lot and he'll survive losing me too.*

"I love you, Dad," I say to his bowed gray head. And pop out.

I wait for Margo in our spot by the river, playing the ukulele under swaying birch branches. I hear her car, watch her get out. She smiles when she sees me, hurries over. The deep brown of her eyes glows chestnut in the sunlight.

"Sleep well?" I ask her.

"Yeah," she says, then realizes that she *actually did*. "*Yeah*," she repeats, amazed. And when she looks at me again, it's begun to dawn on her what this means.

"You're not..." she stammers. "I mean, we can just stay like this, right? Why not?"

I put the ukulele down, step closer to her. "Because you're sixteen and I'm dead," I say.

I was hoping to make her laugh, but she starts to cry.

"We've had more time than most people get," I say, lamely quoting the bartender.

"*No*," she retorts fiercely. "We *haven't*. We were supposed to have a *lifetime* together. It's not fair."

I want to jump in the car with her and drive away, try to escape the bell, the bartender, the staircase, all of it. But I know I can't.

"I think," I say, choking up myself, "I was allowed to stay to help you. But you're safe now. So I have to go."

She's sobbing now, overcome.

I should be allowed to hug her, goddamnit, I think, looking around for the bartender.

Yes, we've gotten a couple of months, but it's *not enough*. I close my eyes and plead silently, desperately: *Please. Just let me kiss her goodbye.*

When I open my eyes again, I see the bartender behind Margo.

"It's time to go," he says stonily.

I cannot bear this. I *can't* leave her this way, hunched over with grief. Not my Margo.

"*Please*, just let me hold her one more time," I beg him.

"Why?" he says. "Why should you get that privilege?"

I look at him, and suddenly I see not just firm authority, but *pain* in his eyes. *He* didn't get that privilege, I realize.

"Did you have a wife?" I ask him. "A lover? You did, didn't you? And you didn't get to say goodbye." A flash of anger darkens his face, but I keep going: "Look, I'm sorry you didn't get that privilege, I really am. But please, *please*, do it for another guy."

He turns away, looks at the river, and for a minute I think I'm going to be popped out then and there. And then I feel Margo in my arms, *really* in my arms, nuzzling my cheek. It's Christmas, Disneyworld, and the Fourth of July all in one. My girl kissing me, holding on to me, my *love*. I clutch her like I've never held her before, kiss her hair.

When she finally pulls back to look at me, I see something in her eyes that clinches it for me: *strength*.

"I'll be okay," she says. Then leans over and whispers in my ear. "And I'll always love you."

And then there's a whir, of color and emotion. Jade green, glistening yellow, love like an ocean. And music, *soaring* music. As I get my bearings, I realize I'm on the staircase. Margo is gone, but knowing she's okay, I'm ready.

With each step upward, a joyous pastiche of mental references flows through my head: it seems like my life plus everyone else's. A New Orleans second line, clapping and dancing... Boyd and me as little kids, running through the sprinkler naked... Neil Armstrong stepping onto the moon... a wonder-struck Japanese kid looking up through a shower of cherry blossoms.

And me and Margo, dancing, laughing, kissing.

Me and Margo. *Forever*.

SIXTY-ONE

MARGO

ctober was a hollow month. As people chattered around me—
How did you figure it out, Margo? When no one else could?—
I just felt numb. And then worse than numb; this stab wound
isn't the only hole in my chest. Now that it's all over, I'm finally
mourning three people I loved.

Some days in October I would just come home from school
and go to bed. Dad got it; he'd just let me lie till dinnertime. As
the two of us moved quietly around the house, we were both
alone and together. Finally taking the long walk towards recovery, each in our own way.

I gave him a gift, one I knew he'd enjoy while simultaneous-
ly chastising me. I told him about Sam's bad soil report, about
him paying off the soil company. He had to tell me off for breaking into the Claypools, but the news also put a little spring in his
step. He got to be a cop again, one with solid evidence against
his lifelong rival.

Delia always seemed to know when I needed her. She'd
come and curl up with me, joke and gossip or just *be* there, silent.

I know Mom was right. I had to let Hank go. And yet the *emptiness* people leave behind when they die, the *quiet*, is just flattening. A cold wind blows through the empty space and you feel like you'll never get warm again.

Something that helps, strangely, is my new relationship with the painting in our living room. I look at it every day now. I don't hate it anymore. In fact, I actually kind of love it. Because the kids in it are just playing now. They're *safe*. It's not a *wound* anymore, the painting Mom liked so much. Now it's like a window to her; somehow I can sense fresh spring air and Mom's perfume flowing at me through it. *So sweet.*

I had a surprise visitor on Halloween. I was sitting on the porch, a bowl of mini candy bars in my lap, determined to be *fun* for the trick-or-treaters. Anyhow, I was lost in the surreal parade of kid skeletons and zombie brides when a lone man appeared: Gib Hawkins. Holding his hat, looking nervously at me. I invited him to sit down. He did and we just sat in silence for a minute.

Dad had gotten him off any charges he may have incurred for bursting into a hospital and aiming a shotgun at a patient. He's officially on probation, but it's pretty meaningless.

After a long pause, he finally said he'd brought something for me. Then reached into his pocket, brought out a cowgirl doll, and handed it to me. I looked at it: cloth, very Southwestern, with a brown fringe vest and skirt, boots, blonde pigtails.

"June and I took a trip once," he explained. "I got this for her in Texas. She gave it back to me when we..." He trailed off, then: "Anyhow, I want you to have it."

I thanked him for the gift, awkwardly resting the doll on top of my candy bars.

After a long minute, he added, softly: "She was a great girl."

"Yes, she was," I agreed.

As we sat and watched the kids run from house to house, I realized I had one more puzzle piece I needed to fit in.

"Did you ever wear a cologne called Chesapeake?" I asked him.

He looked over at me, surprised. "Yes," he said. "June gave it to me. But then, later, I didn't want it anymore, so I gave it to…"

He couldn't even say the name.

"*My son.*" He finally finished.

So that's how she recognized it. I had the piece now, but the moment had soured. Gib got up to leave; I thanked him again for the doll. He nodded and headed out amidst the ghosts and goblins.

For some reason, after Halloween passed and November began, I was ready to join the living again.

I head over to the police station almost every day after school now and do the work June used to do. I even find myself keeping tabs on the town like she did. Yesterday I made a note: *Carolyn Claypool has a dazed look on her face that says: "I almost ran off with a madman." Talk about dodging a bullet.*

I could feel June smiling down on me, amused.

And now it's Thanksgiving. Delia's parents have closed the Dragon House down for a private dinner: just her family, me and Dad, and the Jameses. The first snow of the season is falling as Delia and I arrange dishes on a long table. The Changs have made a combination of traditional American fare and Chinese specialties: turkey and stuffing await us alongside Peking duck and rainbow shrimp. Sinatra's crooning on the sound system (Zhen loves Frank), candles are lit, and faces are bright with holiday cheer. Delia and Boyd are joking around; she seems to be bringing out the wise ass in him. He's not looking at me *that* way anymore, and I'm relieved.

The only solemn note is three empty places Zhen has set for Hank, June, and JoAnn. It's her tradition, setting places for the departed, and I appreciate it. As I take my place at the table, I can feel all three of them with us. The cold wind is gone.

As Dad makes his toast—the same one he makes every year—I run my fingers over a silver bracelet that Hank gave me. *Love always, Hank,* reads the inscription on the inside. Dad finishes up, then adds a new toast to Mom, Hank, and June. As he speaks and we wipe away tears, I can almost see each of them shimmering in their seats.

Finally everyone clinks glasses and digs in. But quietly, to myself, I make my own prayer of thanksgiving to Hank:
Thanks for being here when I needed you. Thanks for being beside me our whole lives. And count on this: I will see you later.

ACKNOWLEDGMENTS

I walked a long road writing this book, but wound up at such a wonderful place: Owl Hollow Press. I couldn't have asked for a better home for *Lazarus*. I'd like to thank everyone at OHP, with special shout-outs to editor extraordinaire Hannah Smith, who made me up my game, Olivia Swenson, who caught mistakes I still can't believe I didn't notice, and Emma Nelson, the OHP maestro who handles everything with such good humor and kindness.

A BIG thank you to my wonderful agent Liza Fleissig, for believing in me and allowing for this Hollywood escapee's second act. And thanks to Julia Benz for helping me find Liza.

Still more enormous thanks to Arthur Schurr, Terry Holzman and Tanya Ward Goodman, for your time, wisdom and notes. I could not have written this book without you.

Thanks to Karol Ruth Silverstein for showing a newbie the ropes.

Thanks to George Melloan, Patricia Woods, Mary Anastasia O'Grady, Jenny Duffy, Wilson Jungerman, Mimi Drop and John Talbot for your thoughts and encouragement.

Additional thanks to Johanna Farrand, Liz Fenton, Joe Bosso, Vivi Mata, Richard Byard, Viva Hardigg, Walter F. Rodriguez and William Lucas Walker—I love yuz all.

And finally, endless thanks to the Melloan, Woods, Duffy and Vandervalk families for your love and support. You guys got me here.

MARYANNE

MELLOAN WOODS

Photo by Sara McKenna Woods

Maryanne Melloan Woods is a novelist, screenwriter, and playwright currently living in the New York area. She received a B.A. in Theatre Arts from Drew University and an M.F.A. in Screenwriting from the American Film Institute in Los Angeles.

As a TV writer/producer, Maryanne has written shows for networks including Showtime, NBC, ABC, Fox, the WB, Nickelodeon and ABC Family.

Maryanne's plays have been produced by HBO's New Writers Project, the Mark Taper Forum, and many theatres around the country. She won the New England Theatre Conference's John Gassner Playwriting Contest and the Venice (CA) Playwrights'

Festival and also received a playwriting grant from the New Jersey State Council on the Arts. Her play, *Smells Like Gin*, was the first play produced by Writers Theatre of New Jersey, and she recently won "Best Comedy Script" in the Nashville Film Festival's screenwriting competition for her screenplay *Steve*.

She has taught screenwriting at the Gotham Writers Workshop in New York, UCLA and the American Film Institute, and served as a panelist for TV writing seminars at NYU and the University of Wisconsin. Maryanne was also a mentor/teacher for The Unusual Suspects, a playwriting workshop for at-risk teens in L.A.

Maryanne Melloan Woods is represented by
Liza Fleissig of Liza Royce Agency.

#LAZARUS | #LAZARUSBOOK